House Arrest

She was old and frail and lived alone, and when they came and told her her roof needed repairing she believed them. She even believed them when they told her it would cost much more than the estimate and they had to have cash down. How could she help believing, when they had taken hostage the most precious thing she had?

It wasn't the end. For her great-niece it was the beginning of a do-it-yourself detective job. Dissatisfied with police progress in what had become a murder investigation, the young woman began making inquiries of her own. Aided by a journalist friend, she uncovered evidence which left her in no doubt of the identity of the criminals, but proof was something else. From do-it-yourself detection to do-it-yourself justice seemed a small step—but it had momentous consequences.

by the same author

THE SECOND TIME IS EASY
DEAD HEAT
PRIME TARGET
THE DARKER SIDE OF DEATH
CENSOR
A DOMESTIC AFFAIR
THE SEARCH FOR SARA
ALL PART OF THE SERVICE
RAINBLAST
BACKLASH
CATSPAW
DEATH FUSE
TOUCHDOWN
A DANGEROUS PLACE TO DWELL
DAYLIGHT ROBBERY
DIAL DEATH
MR T
DOUBLE DEAL
MURDER BY THE MILE
THE CLIENT
PHANTOM HOLIDAY
CRIME WAVE
DOUBLE HIT
CONCRETE EVIDENCE
ADVISORY SERVICE
DEADLINE
HUNT TO A KILL
DANGER MONEY
NO RETURN TICKET
NO THROUGH ROAD

MARTIN RUSSELL

House Arrest

COLLINS, 8 GRAFTON STREET, LONDON W1

William Collins Sons & Co. Ltd
London · Glasgow · Sydney · Auckland
Toronto · Johannesburg

First published 1988
© Martin Russell 1988

British Library Cataloguing in Publication Data

Russell, Martin
   House arrest.—(Crime Club)
   I. Title
   823'.914[F]

   ISBN 0 00 232182 3

Photoset in Linotron Baskerville by
Rowland Phototypesetting Ltd
Bury St Edmunds, Suffolk
Printed in Great Britain by
William Collins Sons & Co. Ltd, Glasgow

CHAPTER 1

Maisie liked the look of the man standing inside her porch. Although he wasn't quite smiling, his head was tilted slightly in the way that she had always been inclined to trust: the benevolent slant of the physician. I'm here, it said, to help you. In one hand the man was holding a briefcase; in the other, a card on which something was printed, though without her glasses Maisie couldn't make out what it said. Alongside the print there was a smudgy photograph. Before she could produce her spectacles case, he had returned the card to a pocket of his natty jacket—suede, it looked like— and increased still further his cranial list.

'Good *morning*, madam. Am I addressing the lady of the house?'

'You're not talking to the butler,' she assured him with a certain amused asperity, fastening the top button of her cardigan before stepping out to join him in the porch. Everyone said you shouldn't—Anita, her great-niece, would have had fifty fits—but any dolt could see with half an eye that this caller was all right. Besides which, it was ten-thirty, broad daylight, a weekday: people were up and about, or if they weren't they should be, and in the event of trouble there would be no shortage of aid. Defying all indications to the contrary, Maisie maintained her obstinate faith in the moral probity of the nation. 'I suppose,' she added, arching her neck to look up at him, 'you've got something you want to sell?'

'That's it, madam. Peace of mind. This is what we have on offer today.'

'You're one of those Bible-pushers?'

'I wouldn't knock such people,' he returned gravely.

'Their motivation is beyond reproach. As ours is, I hope. We want to save you trouble. It's about your roof.'

'Roof?' Maisie peered vaguely through the porch skylight. 'What about the roof?'

'Did you know that parts of it are . . . shall we say, not as robust as they might be?'

'Oh dear.' Stepping past him on to the gravelled drive, she stood shivering a little in the April gusts, gazing upwards at a blurred image of gables and drainpipes. 'What's the matter with it?'

He joined her to point with a gloved finger. 'Faulty slating, for starters. Plus a suspected timber problem underneath. Until we get up there, of course, we shan't know for certain.'

Maisie lowered her gaze to look at him. 'Who's "we"?' she demanded.

'The company I represent. We're conducting a survey of structural deficiencies in the area. I've taken a look at your ridge and gulleys through the binoculars and I'm sorry to say, my dear, it all seems to need quite a lot of attention.'

'I see.' Maisie paused while she came to terms with this sudden disagreeable item of news. 'I'd no idea. Since my husband died I've not had anyone round to see to the . . . What sort of work is needed? Will it cost much, do you think?'

'We'll do all that we can to keep the price down for you.' He reminded Maisie irresistibly of Dr Parker explaining the minimum number of daily tablets that would do the trick for her arthritis. 'As I say, until we get a closer look at the damage I can't make any firm promises, but this I can guarantee—you won't be committed to any needless expenditure. Mind you,' he added, stepping back a pace to re-examine the sky and using his other gloved hand to shield his eyes from the watery spring glare, 'I should emphasize that we do have a statutory duty to ensure that all building fabric is maintained to a standard that precludes danger to the general public. I know you'll appreciate that.'

'Oh, of course.' Maisie's grasp of his meaning was some-what tenuous, but she did infer that it was something too important to ignore. 'I wouldn't want to run any risk. Besides, it's . . . it's an investment, isn't it? The house, I mean. Worth keeping up to scratch.'

'Madam,' he informed her solemnly, 'I can see that I don't have to explain things to you in tedious detail. You've obviously worked them out for yourself.' Producing from his briefcase a dainty pair of binoculars, the caller placed them to his eyes and swept the guttering with them. To Maisie he seemed young. Not more than fifty, and still with plenty of hair. A sandy thatch with a wave in it, not unlike her Billy's. But for that stupid drunken driver, Billy would now have been just about this man's age. A similar build, too. Slim, with an upright stance. Maisie had taught Billy how to hold himself. She never could abide men who stooped.

Laryngeal sounds, suggestive of dubiety, were emerging from the throat of her visitor. With an abruptly decisive movement he restored the binoculars to the briefcase and swung to face her again. 'I'll be quite frank with you, Mrs . . .?'

'Holwood.'

'You do have a problem there, Mrs Holwood. One Force Seven gale is all it would take.'

'You mean . . . things might blow off it?'

'It's not really a question of *might*. To be quite candid with you, what it needs, that roof of yours, is immediate attention by trained specialists, otherwise . . .'

Maisie blinked up at him. 'Otherwise?'

'You're going to be liable for any harm that might be caused. Tell me something, Mrs Holwood. What third-party accident provision is there on your property insurance, d'you happen to know?'

She gawped in silent dismay. Her knowledge of insurance

could have been inscribed quite legibly on the back of a postage stamp by a child with a marker pen. Presently she said, 'I'm afraid I . . . Mr Farrell sees to all that for me.'

'Mr Farrell?' the caller repeated alertly.

'The gentleman three doors away. When the insurance people send me a reminder I just take it in to him and he sees to everything. I'm not sure what it . . . what it . . .'

'Perhaps you'd like to ask him?'

'Oh no. I wouldn't want to put him to any trouble. He'd be at the office now, in any case. We're not on close terms. It's just that he's always done it for me, once a year, since my husband died. It's quite a good insurance, I believe. They're a well-known firm. My husband always dealt with them.'

'Still, it's highly doubtful if you'd be covered for the sort of damage or injury that could be caused by structural disintegration resulting from neglect,' the man said fluently, snapping the hasps of his briefcase. 'I tell you what, Mrs Holwood. My business associates are in the neighbourhood, as it happens. They're attending to a block of flats along by the church. Flat roof problems, needless to say. But they're pretty well finished, so they could make your property their next port of call, so to speak. Run the ladder up, inspect the slating and roof struts, let us know what's required. Then we needn't waste any time getting something done about it. What do you say?'

'It's very kind of you.' Maisie felt a trifle dizzy. She groped her way back to the porch. 'If there are things that want doing, I suppose it's only sensible . . . It's the cost I'm worried about. I can't afford a big outlay.'

From the drive, he said soothingly, 'Now don't you go getting yourself all worked up on that score, Mrs Holwood. Trust us. We'll come to some workable arrangement.'

*

The business associates arrived twenty minutes later in a small van with ladders on the roof-rack.

Neither of them was the giant of a man that Maisie had vaguely expected. One, slightly the less inscrutable of the pair, was barely taller than herself, and a lot bonier: he looked as if he could do with a few square meals. He seemed to be in his forties. The other, although strongly built, was no colossus. He did, however, give out an impression of power and agility, accentuated by his youth: Maisie put his age at no more than twenty-five. In combination, she supposed, their specialist expertise was sufficient to compensate for any lack of inches. Certainly they seemed efficient. Without any exchange of words, up went an aluminium ladder and up its rungs scuttled Bony, who from gutter level gave the roof an inspection lasting fifteen seconds—the time it took Ouncey to absorb his main meal of the day before glancing around for more—before descending rapidly, shaking his head. Maisie regarded him anxiously. The man with the binoculars gave her left arm a bracing squeeze, scrunched across the gravel to meet him.

'Well, Percy? What's the verdict?'

Percy muttered something. His partner, who was holding the base of the ladder, rubbed the side of his nose reflectively. With a nod, the spokesman of the trio rotated on his heels and returned to where Maisie stood, clutching the cardigan across herself where the buttons were missing.

'I'm sorry, Mrs Holwood, to have to say so, but it does appear that I was right.'

'Fairly bad, is it?' she asked faintly.

'Put it this way. If it were left for another month, we couldn't be answerable for the consequences. Not that it will be left, of course. We've a statutory commitment to make it safe.'

'Yes, I see.'

'At the same time, my dear, nobody wants to cause you

financial embarrassment. We do realize this has come a bit out of the blue.'

'If it needs doing, I shall just have to find the money.'

'Spoken like a trouper, Mrs Holwood, if I may say so. Percy and Dave here will do all in their power to minimize the operation, you can depend on that. At the same time . . .'

He paused. Maisie stared up at him imploringly.

'I should warn you,' he resumed with an air of diffidence, 'that until they start stripping off to the rafters they can't actually specify what they'll be needing in terms of labour-duration and materials and the like. You can understand that.'

'Whatever's wanted,' Maisie said miserably, 'they'll have to get, I dare say.'

'That's the sensible way of looking at it.'

'I just want the work done.'

'Naturally you do. Until you've a good, sound roof over your head, you won't sleep peacefully at nights, am I right? Well, Mrs Holwood, I'll tell you something. We're going to see to it that you get one. Now then. When would you like us to start?'

'When *can* you start?'

He turned to the other two, standing like zombies at the foot of the ladder. 'Finished at the apartment block, lads? Then can we make Mrs Holwood top priority? Grade A service, tidy everything up for her with no delay?'

Wordlessly, Percy and Dave stumped away to the van and began hauling out equipment. To Maisie it seemed a hotch-potch, but she supposed they knew what they were up to. The firm's mouthpiece took a gentle grip of her arm.

'While they're making a start, Mrs Holwood, shall we just be sorting out the financial aspect? What we *don't* want is for you to be having nightmares over it. If a system of graduated payments is likely to be of any assistance . . .'

'That won't be necessary,' Maisie said with some sharpness. 'I can pay for what's needed.'

'You're a sound manager, I can see that. Tell you what, my love. If we were to step indoors for five minutes, we could go through the figures, come to some understanding right away. Then you'll know near enough where you stand. How does that strike you?'

'I thought you said you wouldn't have much idea till you'd stripped the roof?'

'Right. But we can lay down some approximate guidelines. Hourly rates, basic material costs. Don't look so worried, my love. We shan't let it rise above what's fair and reasonable, having regard to the state of affairs as we find them. Take no notice of the hammering. It's only Dave, checking out the timberwork. Thorough lad, is Dave. Conscientious to a fault. Used to be a house painter before he came over to me, so he's at home with heights. Percy pulls his weight, too, what there is of it. You probably noticed . . . Now this, Mrs Holwood, is very nice. Very nice indeed. I do like your wallpaper. High ceilings, too. Lots of headroom. Takes some looking after, I'll bet, a place like this. Have someone in, do you, most days?'

'I do my own housework,' Maisie said proudly, taking a fresh look at her hall. 'Always have. Never did like people fussing round me.'

'Good on you, my love. Independence, they call it. A fast-vanishing attribute. Which way—along here? Still, you've got your family to fall back on, I expect.'

'My niece is very good. Great-niece, I should say. She looks in on me from time to time. Brings me all the news.'

'That's nice. Anybody else?'

'They've all gone,' Maisie said simply. 'I'm the last.'

'Dear me. What about the neighbours? Don't they come calling?'

'Oh, I don't like to trouble them. Ouncey and I get along

all right.' Throwing open the door to what she called the sitting-room, Maisie stood aside to make way. 'Apart from Anita,' she informed him, 'you're the first caller I've had for months.'

'You're kidding?'

'No, it's the truth. That's why Ouncey's making that silly noise. He's not used to visitors. All right, Ouncey, quiet now. Good boy. Come along and say hullo nicely to . . .'

'Nigel,' supplied her companion, stepping cautiously into the room. 'Hi there, Ouncey. *You're* a handsome little fellow, and no mistake.'

'He needs a good brushing,' Maisie said fondly.

The advance of the Yorkshire terrier across the threadbare carpet was accomplished in a series of starts and pauses, with an occasional yap to test the atmosphere until dog and visitor were tentatively in contact, nose to knuckle. 'I can see,' Nigel observed, essaying a pat or two which the dog eluded, 'why your missus dotes on *you*. Look after her, do you? Keep her company?'

'Without Ouncey,' declared Maisie, stooping to pick him up, 'I couldn't exist. He's everything to me.'

'Aha. So that's all you need do for a living—right, Ouncey? Just be yourself. How old is he?'

'He'll be six in July.'

'Prime of his doggy life.' Nigel stood looking at him. 'Must be a great comfort to you, Mrs Holwood. Knowing he'll still be around, I mean, for a good few years yet. Good life-span, have they?'

'He'll see me out, I shouldn't wonder.'

With a final vague gesture in the dog's direction, Nigel walked over to the elderly, scarred dining table in a corner of the room and dumped his briefcase on the stained sepia cloth with which it was covered. From the case he produced a clipboard which he laid down face-up; from his breast pocket he unclipped a ballpen. 'Now then,' he said on a businesslike note, resting both palms on the table edge and gazing down meditatively. 'Age of structure . . . Late Victorian? Turn of the century?'

'The house?' Maisie relinquished the dog, who trotted back to his heap of bedding in another corner, next to an oil stove of antiquated design. 'It dates from 1909,' she volunteered with the precision of total certainty. 'My late husband's grandfather built it, as a matter of fact. Along with the next three down the street. He was in the trade.'

'You don't say?' Nigel gave the room an admiring survey. 'Knew how to build, didn't they, in those days? Solid as rock. Shame the years have to catch up, in the end. If you'll just hang on a minute, Mrs Holwood, while I scribble down a few figures . . .'

Maisie watched him apprehensively. Before his arrival, she had been wondering about a new woolly cardigan to see her through the chilly weeks that undoubtedly remained to be surmounted: now, it was beginning to look as though anything so frivolous would have to be relegated to the Pending file, which lately was showing signs of bursting at the seams. Did it matter? What did she want with a new garment? Only Ouncey was here to see her, and sartorially speaking his eye was not critical. As long as he was fed and fussed over, he wouldn't care if she padded around the house in a potato sack.

'Couple of hundred for the labour,' Nigel announced, straightening suddenly and discarding the ballpen. 'Estimated figure, assuming no complications. Allowing for contingencies, let's say two-fifty. Then you've got—'

'Two hundred and fifty pounds?'

'That's it, my love. Told you, didn't I, we'd keep it within strict limits?'

'It seems . . . rather a lot of money.'

Nigel looked a little hurt. 'If you can find someone cheaper,' he said mildly, 'you're welcome to give 'em a call.

Fetch 'em along, get a quotation out of 'em. I sincerely wish
you luck. My estimate—'

'I'm quite sure,' Maisie said hurriedly, 'you're as reasonable as anybody else. It's just a bit unexpected, that's all. I
thought it was only a few slates.'

'I did mention the timbers,' he reminded her. 'But we
won't anticipate the worst. We'll have the verdict from Dave
shortly. Stay cool, my love. Whatever happens, I'll work
something out for you.'

'I know you will.'

'Keep in mind, though, it's labour costs only I've given
you thus far. Materials could be something else. But let's
not rush our fences. That Dave I can hear? Sounds like
someone in the porch. I'll tell him to come through.'

Nigel vanished into the hall. Hobbling painfully to her
favourite chair, Maisie lowered herself into it. From here,
she purposely was unable to see the french window or the
shrubbery and beeches beyond: the sight of her unkempt
quarter of an acre was one that she could live without. It
was too depressing a reminder of her inability to cope with
the property. She should sell up, she supposed, as Anita was
always urging her to do. Move into Sheltered Accommo-
dation. Maisie shuddered. The mere thought was enough
to chill her blood.

Returning from his bed, Ouncey sprang on to the chair
beside her and from there progressed to her lap, giving her
twisted fingers a couple of licks before settling himself into
the warm ball that soothed her thighs like a hot-water bottle
with a mind of its own. After a sigh, Ouncey dozed off. She
sat tickling his ears.

Two hundred and fifty pounds. Not counting the materials. Plus whatever else they might find while they were
up there. The jolt was a severe one, the biggest she had
experienced for a year or more. But if the work was vital . . .

Nigel returned with Dave in tow. Nigel was straight-faced.

'Got some rather gloomy news for you, Mrs Holwood, I'm afraid.'

She said tremulously, 'What is it?'

'Rot.'

She stared at him, bewildered.

Coming forward, he sat on the rim of the table. 'Seems you've a problem,' he enlarged, 'with damp decay under that roof of yours. *Quite* a problem, unfortunately. Dave's had a good look and he reckons it's going to mean some extra stripping down. Something we hadn't bargained on.'

'More expense?' Maisie asked faintly.

'We'll do all in our power to keep it down for you. Place your faith in us, my love. We're on your side.'

'Yes, but how much is it all going to come to?' Maisie felt giddy. She wanted this awful hour or two to end: life to get back on course. Dazedly she watched Nigel pull a chair out from beneath the table, install himself, get solemnly to work with his pen and his clipboard. Taking up station by the wall, the phlegmatic Dave stood with arms folded across his chest, gazing expressionlessly at Ouncey as if assessing the dog for incipient corrosion. After a while, Nigel began to mumble to himself.

'Trade price, less discount . . . should fetch it down a bit . . . minimum hourly rate, weekday working . . .'

CHAPTER 2

The van bounced like a sprung mattress, rattled like a carelessly-packed tool chest. Nigel drove with flamboyance. Approaching junctions repeatedly at full speed, he applied the brakes each time at the last half-second, causing traffic on the major road to veer in expectation of catastrophe.

After the first such incident, Maisie closed her eyes and kept them shut.

'High Street?' he inquired, making her jump. 'By the supermarket, you said?'

'Yes. You can park on the forecourt.'

'Got your passbook at the ready?'

'In my bag.'

'You're a good manager, Mrs Holwood, I can see that. Always something in reserve for emergencies.'

Too dispirited to reply, Maisie shut her eyes again, trusting to the seat-harness to hold her in place. When finally she reopened them, Nigel was shooting the lights at the entrance to High Street and about to run down a knot of people on a pedestrian crossing. She glanced away. Somehow tragedy was averted. Recovering her poise, she was able to direct him to the building society premises next to the Smartshop Foodstore, which she patronized once a fortnight for grocery essentials and offal for Ouncey. She never stayed long. The town as a whole bore no resemblance now to the provincial village that she and Eric had found so restful when they first moved into the area, long before the Second World War. Progress had laid clammy hands on the district: no longer had it anything to offer her.

The building society branch, however, had altered little. Nervously applying her six stone to its spring-loaded glass door, she battled through to the over-warmed interior and joined the queue of investors who, passbooks in hand, were waiting at the rope barrier for service.

Information on interest rates and mortgage availability was plastered everywhere. While Maisie was eyeing it with less than total comprehension, Nigel came in to take up position at her elbow.

'Found a space,' he said sunnily. 'You can take your time, Mrs Holwood. Lot of people here, aren't there, wanting their money. Speaking of which, I'm assuming you'll be drawing yours by cash *and* cheque?'

'Do you think I should?'

'Two-fifty quid limit on cash withdrawals. You're going to need more than that. So what I'd suggest, if I may, is that you take out that amount in banknotes plus a cheque for the balance, made payable to me . . . save hassle, won't it? Then I can pay it direct into the firm's account.'

'I see.'

'Once we're funded, we can lay in the materials and get cracking on that minor disaster of a roof of yours. Make sense?'

'If that's what you think is best.' Maisie was squinting at the last page of entries inside the passbook, which she had managed to retrieve from its special hiding place at home while Nigel and Dave were in debate in the hall. She didn't mind Nigel, but somehow she hadn't wanted Dave to know of its whereabouts. Although she recognized its value, Maisie was vagueness itself about the mechanics of running such an account. Eric had always dealt with such matters. Knowing he was a keen saver, she had always been content to leave it to him. Since his death, she had made no use of the money at all, subconsciously regarding it as a kind of pension fund in reserve: for day-to-day expenses she scraped by on her State pension and the small private one from the insurance company to which Eric had contributed. 'I hope there's enough to cover it,' she added, blinking hard in an attempt to sharpen the blur in which the passbook entries were surrounded. She handed the book over to him. 'Can you read what it says?'

Nigel examined it respectfully. 'Six thousand, eight-seventy,' he reported in a reverent undertone. 'Plus a few odd pennies. That include the interest to date, Mrs Holwood?'

'Oh yes.' This was one, at least, that she could answer.

'I've had the book made up every year. Eric—my husband told me always to do that.'

'Nice, tidy sum,' he complimented her, returning the passbook. 'And you couldn't spend it in a better cause, my love. House maintenance.'

'I suppose not.' Maisie glanced up at him trustingly. More and more he reminded her of Billy: he had the same trick of resting featherlight against her, maintaining shoulder-to-thigh body contact without any of the irritating dabs and pokes that less desirable people were apt to scatter around like tawdry accessories to otherwise acceptable garb. 'So what shall I ask them,' she inquired, 'to make the cheque out for?'

Nigel cogitated. 'What was it we estimated? Six-ninety? With an allowance for unforeseeable extras, say seventy-five in round terms. So it's two-fifty in cash, and five hundred above your signature, Mrs Holwood, if you'd be so kind. Leaving you still with a good, round figure to pay for that world cruise you'll be taking this summer.'

Maisie sniffed. 'World cruise. Ouncey would have something to say if I went off and left him. Anyway, dry land's good enough for me, thank you very much.'

'I agree with you,' Nigel said earnestly. 'When you've a bit of capital behind you, why spend it on something you . . . Cashier available. There you go. Under the flashing green light. I'll wait by the door.'

The reaction of the girl to a withdrawal request was one of impassivity. Without knowing what to expect, Maisie had braced herself for a slight frown, possibly a suppressed tut-tut: perhaps even a polite demand to be told what she wanted to do with the money. The reality was almost anti-climax. No sooner had she asked, than a blend of ten- and twenty-pound notes came at her beneath the glass screen, closely pursued by the passbook in which was tucked a rectangular document the size of a holiday brochure which proved to be the cheque, made out to N. J. Murphy—the name Nigel had given her—and signed in extravagant script on behalf of the society, which had debited the account accordingly. It now stood at six thousand, one hundred and twenty pounds, plus the few odd pennies.

Maisie felt a sense of relief. The sum was barely altered from what it had been before, and yet now she was in a position to pay three men—specialists—to put the roof over her head into prime condition for years to come. Lightheartedly she rejoined Nigel. He smiled down at her, so heartbreakingly in Billy's style that all her ribs seemed to twist and reset themselves inside her chest.

'Transaction completed, my love? Let's get back, then.'

Bravely ignoring the fact that the return journey was no less hair-raising, Maisie this time kept her eyes resolutely open and asked questions about Nigel's career. His answers were frank and entertaining, heavily larded with comic anecdote. The odd thing was, by the time they reached the house she knew no more about him, or the firm he represented, than she had when he first set foot inside her porch. Not that she minded. Maisie understood about reticence. She was that way inclined herself. Ouncey was the one pair of ears in which she confided: he was always sympathetic, and never made demands.

From the drive there was no sign of Dave or Percy, who when they left had been securing the ladder and assembling tools. Assisting Maisie out of the van, Nigel glanced up at the roof. 'Shame to waste this dry spell,' he observed. 'Tell you what. We've a few odd slates in the back of the van, so I'll get the lads on the job right away. Leave you in peace again by the day after tomorrow, I shouldn't wonder.'

'As soon as that?'

'Ah, we don't mess about, Mrs Holwood, once we've got our teeth into something. Let's go and find them, shall we? I've a shrewd notion they might be sampling the comforts of your living-room furniture—very taken with that sofa of yours, Dave was, I could see that with half an eye. They won't take advantage,' he assured her with a squeeze of an arm. 'Couple of good blokes, they are. Genuine workers. They won't disappoint you.'

As predicted, both men were deeply established in the upholstery of their choice when Maisie and Nigel re-entered the living-room. Percy had opted for the basketwork rocker which Maisie herself occasionally occupied, as a change from her leather-bound favourite, when she wanted to watch the television . . . and in which she had once or twice found herself slumped when she awoke, still fully dressed, at two in the morning with no recollection of having drowsed off in mid-programme. It fitted Percy, who looked ready to lie back in it for the rest of the day. He was welcome to it, she told herself, for twenty minutes. As for Dave, if he liked to sample briefly a full-length posture on the grunting sofa with its padded end that served nicely as a headrest, she didn't begrudge him that pleasure, either. So long as they did a good job on her roof. Something was missing, though. She peered short-sightedly about the room.

'Where's Ouncey? Did he ask to go in the garden?'

Neither man seemed to hear. Behind her, Nigel said briskly, 'Come on, lads. You heard Mrs Holwood. What's become of the little fellow?'

Both gave slight shakes of the head. Their combined muteness was unnerving: confronted by it continuously, Maisie thought, she would have gone off her head in a week. Nigel evidently was used to it. Overtaking her, he went to the french door and thrust it open. He whistled on two notes.

'Here, boy. Din-dins. Come and get it.'

'He doesn't get fed,' Maisie informed the room, 'until I have my own lunch.'

For some reason her heart had started to beat heavily and

erratically, as it sometimes did after a richer meal than usual or when she had over-exerted herself with the carpet-sweeper. To calm it, she began to inhale deeply while sitting with outward nonchalance on an upright chair at the table, the cloth of which was still strewn with Nigel's stationery.

'Ouncey,' she called. 'Where are you, treasure? Come to Mummy.'

No answering scuffle reached her ears. She raised her voice to a sharper pitch. 'Come on, now. Don't be unsociable. We've got visitors.'

'He'd sooner see the back of us,' Nigel said jovially. Closing the french door, he glanced from Dave to Percy. 'One of you must have seen him. Did he go out of the room?'

From his recumbent position on the sofa, Dave gazed out at the garden. Percy coughed throatily. 'Never noticed the little beggar, quite honestly. Maybe he's under the table.'

'He never goes under the table.' Maisie spoke with fortitude that she was far from feeling. Everything inside her, from knees to stomach, had started to wobble. Breathing was increasingly difficult. Luckily Nigel, bless him, rescued her from further vocal effort.

'Now, you blokes, this just isn't good enough. While we were out, Mrs Holwood's pet was your responsibility. He can't have wandered off, just like that. So where's he got to?'

Dave stretched himself lazily, producing groans from the sofa. 'We might've seen him.'

Nigel looked at him. 'What's that supposed to mean?'

'She want him back, does she?'

'If you're alluding to our client here, Mrs Holwood, I'll thank you to make use of the lady's name. Where were you dragged up, Dave Forester? Naturally Mrs Holwood wants Ouncey back.'

Dave investigated his palms.

'Well?' demanded Nigel.

Presently he turned back to Maisie. 'Don't worry, my love. Leave this with me. You'll have Ouncey back before you can say Doggybix. Might he be elsewhere in the house?'

'The kitchen, perhaps.' Maisie gasped the words. Wanting to rise from the chair, go off in search herself, she found herself not up to the task: all strength had drained out of her. If only somebody else were here. Anita would have known what to do. How to handle the situation. But what *was* the situation? Maisie couldn't be sure. All she knew was, her heartbeat was violent as never before, and she couldn't move her legs.

Nigel turned to Percy. 'Hear that, Perce? Mrs Holwood thinks her Yorkie may be in the kitchen.'

'Why don't she go and take a look?'

'If you were any sort of a gentleman, you'd save her the bother.'

'Yeah, well. I'm feeling a bit tired.'

'You'll have to accept my apologies, Mrs Holwood, on behalf of my colleagues. Dave, I'm surprised at you. I thought you'd have been out of this door by now, exploring the kitchen on behalf of our client. What's keeping you?'

Dave placed his arms behind his neck. 'No need,' he said.

'No need? You mean you know where the dog is?'

Dave looked at him inscrutably. Nigel released a low hissing sound. 'It's not very nice for Mrs Holwood, hearing all this woolly talk. If you do know anything, she's a right to be told.'

'She can have the dog back. When we're good and ready.'

After a pause, Nigel turned again to Maisie. 'Dave likes to have his little joke. Stay with us, my love. He'll start talking sense in a minute.'

'She can have him . . .' Pivoting on a hip, Dave swung both feet to the floor, sat round in a hunched, reflective attitude. '. . . when she settles the account. How about that?'

'Oh, now Dave. Is that reasonable?'

The younger man said nothing. From the rocker, Percy remarked, 'It's business.'

'Mrs Holwood's not going to welsh on us. Are you, my love? She's an honest, upright lady—anyone can see that.'

Dave's shoulders rose and fell. 'She wants a job done on her roof, she owes us collateral. Only fair.'

Nigel gestured appealingly in Maisie's direction. 'See what I have to contend with? Good lads, both of 'em, but they do tend to get hold of these funny ideas. You try persuading them, Mrs Holwood . . . I can't.'

'Persuade them?' she stammered.

'Somehow or another, they seem to have latched on to this idea that after we've finished the work you're not going to come across with the money. You and I both know that's nonsense, don't we?'

'You've got the money,' Maisie said feebly.

'Hear that, Dave, Perce? We've got the money.'

'We've an advance payment.'

'It's the full amount,' Maisie protested, anger strengthening her voice. 'That's the price we agreed.'

'Price we agreed,' Nigel reminded Dave.

Dave's rather full lips parted to emit a faint scoffing sound. 'Where'd she get her roof fixed for that?'

'Matter for further negotiation,' Percy put in supportively.

'Come off it, you blokes. Mrs Holwood can't afford fancy figures.'

Dave leaned back against the end of the sofa. 'Only what the job takes. Can't say fairer.'

Nigel pondered. Returning presently to where Maisie sat, he lowered himself to his haunches to gaze into her face.

'Seems we have a slight problem here, Mrs Holwood. As I say, these are good lads. Experienced. If they both say the job's likely to cost more, we need to give weight to their

argument. Having said that, to strike a balance, to be fair
to both sides—'

'All I want is my Ouncey back. I want him, please.'

'You shall *have* him. No need to get into a state over it.
All we have to do is arrive at a figure, acceptable to both
parties.'

'How much more do you want?'

'How much, Dave? Rough estimate?'

'Depends.'

'On what?'

'Sundry items.'

'Can't we give Mrs Holwood some inkling?'

Percy said brightly, 'Why not t'other way round?'

'How do you mean?'

'Why don't *she* tell *us* what she's . . . willing to afford?'

'Could be a possible solution,' Nigel conceded. He placed
a hand on Maisie's right knee, which recoiled. 'Hear that,
my love? What Percy's come up with? Try making us an
offer.'

'I don't know what to say . . .'

'Wish I could help you. It's young Dave here: he's the
boy raising difficulties. There again, as I've explained, I
have to defer to his expertise. He and Percy, they're the
active servicemen as you might say—the blokes at the sharp
end. So naturally they're entitled to their say. Neither of
them—'

'Do they have to hide Ouncey away while we decide?'

'All right, is he, Dave? Got the little fellow somewhere
safe?'

'He's okay. Long as she don't argue too much.'

'Mrs Holwood's not arguing.'

'I don't want to argue. I just want Ouncey back. I'll pay
anything. Whatever you say.'

'Now, my love, let's not be hasty. Can't give us more than
you've got, can you?'

'How much *has* she got?'

Nigel turned his head in rebuke. 'Questions like that, Dave, don't belong in civilized society. It's for our client here to decide. She's not to be hassled.'

Maisie fumbled in her bag. 'You can have the lot.'

'We wouldn't want to take your last cent. Why don't you—'

'It doesn't matter. Ouncey's the one who matters.' With shaking fingers, Maisie lugged the building society passbook from the depths of her bag, slapped it down on the table. 'Have a look. I can't remember . . . See for yourselves.'

'Tell you what.' Reaching for the passbook, Nigel collected it delicately between thumb and forefinger, dangled it while he considered. 'Why don't we settle for a round figure that'll cover our outgoings and still leave room for manœuvre on both sides? Dave? All right by you? Perce?'

'Go ahead.'

'No objections to a good old British compromise? Here we go, then. Here's what I suggest. Three thousand to cover the job and hopefully leave a margin of error. That won't break the bank, will it, Mrs Holwood?'

'As far as I'm concerned, you can have the—'

'And the best of it is,' Nigel continued smoothly, 'it'll still leave you a couple of hundred in hand for a rainy day.' Sliding the passbook into an inside pocket, he straightened up with an audible cracking of knees. 'Sounds like the logical option to me. You get Ouncey back. We cover our overheads. *Your* overheads, ha ha. Strike you as fair and reasonable? In all the circumstances. I doubt if we can do better. Dave, Perce? What's the verdict?'

Dave stayed propped against the sofa's siderest, surveying the garden. After an interval he said, 'Might do the trick. With full trade discount.'

The rocker creaked a little as Percy settled back, his mouth stretched at the corners.

CHAPTER 3

On the way back into town, Nigel's mood was paternal.

'See, my love, where Dave's concerned I have to box a bit clever. If I'd let on how much you really have in your account, Dave would have insisted on the lot. It's not that he's avaricious. It's just his nature. All the time, he's taking the cautious view. Terrified of being overspent, running into debt.'

'Does he like dogs?' Maisie implored her voice not to quiver: as usual it defied her.

Nigel sucked in his cheeks. 'Without describing him as your typical British animal-doctor, I'd call him fair-minded. He only wants Ouncey for the time being: for security. Just until he gets his money.'

'But will he look after him?'

'I'll make sure he does.'

'Do you know where he's keeping him?'

Nigel threw her a boyish, lopsided grin. 'Can't be far, can he? We were only gone half an hour. Dave's all right, my love. Left here, isn't it? And then straight on to the lights. He only gets nasty if he reckons he's being ripped off. Play fair with him, he'll play fair with you.'

'But does he *know* anything about dogs? Ouncey needs his tablets, you see.' The invention had come to Maisie in an inspired flash. 'Two at each mealtime. Otherwise he—'

'Give the bottle to me, my love. I'll pass it on to Dave, see that he gets the little chappie to take 'em.'

'Couldn't you get him back for me, Nigel? You must know where Dave has put him.'

'I'd love to, darling, but you've got to remember—I have my working relationship with the boys to consider. We're a team. That's the only way we can operate.'

'But is the roof really going to cost all this?'

'Six thousand? Could be more . . . who knows?' Nigel stamped the car to a halt at the lights. 'This I promise. If there's an overrun, we'll stand the deficit. What do you say to that?'

'*Three* thousand, you said.'

'That was for Dave's and Percy's benefit.' Nigel chuckled over the wheel. 'What they don't know can't hurt 'em, can it? Protection for you, Mrs Holwood, that was. Far as they're concerned, three thousand represents the limit of your cash resources, and that's the way it's going to stay.'

'I see,' Maisie said blankly.

'But I want you to draw the six.' Letting in the clutch, Nigel aimed the car at the heels of a late-crossing pedestrian, missing them by centimetres. 'All by cheque, made payable again to me.'

'But—'

'Soon as it's cleared and credited to my account, I can call on it for expenses. Pay for the work as it goes along.'

Maisie's head spun, as it used to at school when the arithmetic teacher hit her with opaque calculations from the blackboard. 'What if it goes over the three thousand?'

'You'll get a full refund of any balance.'

'You have to wait,' she said desperately, 'before you can use any of the money. You can't start drawing on it at once.'

'I know that.'

'So in the meantime, I shan't get Ouncey back?' Maisie heard her voice crack. She swallowed fiercely. 'He gets lonesome, you know. He'll pine.'

'He'll have company. Dave will be looking after him, don't forget.'

'What about when he's working?'

'Proper old fusspot, aren't you?' Nigel said playfully. 'There's always the lunch-hour. Dave can get back to him, see he's all right. Or get one of his mates to stand in. Stop *worrying*, my love. Everything's going to run like clockwork. Here we are, back at the portals. Hop inside and be doing the needful while I find some place to leave the car. Don't forget—six thousand payable to N. J. Murphy, same as before. Be with you in a couple of minutes.'

The cashier gave Maisie a second glance when she pushed the passbook through with a whispered request. It was the same girl who had attended to her an hour or so ago; a triangular-faced brunette in her early twenties, with glossed lips and square-rimmed spectacles. At their first contact, she had seemed to take no notice whatever of Maisie. This time, the procedure was less mechanical. Having conned the passbook, the girl glanced up with a conspiratorial smile.

'Changed your mind, have you?'

Maisie gaped at her. 'What did you say?'

'You were in before, weren't you? A short while back. To make a withdrawal.'

'That's right, dear.' Maisie took a shuddering breath in a bid to steady her voice. 'I've . . . had another expense come up. One of those mornings.'

'Lucky it's an immediate access account.' Disconcertingly, the girl seemed to be taking a personal interest in Maisie, the transaction, the whole gloriously convenient set-up offered by the institution for which she had the privilege of working. She eyed the passbook again. 'N. J. Murphy, you said? Same payee as before?'

'That's right, dear.'

'Thought I remembered the name.'

'Will there be any problem?'

'No problem.' Instead of getting on with it, however, the girl continued to study the passbook, now and then aiming further glances past discreetly doctored eyelashes at Maisie, who strove to look nonchalant. Presently she added, 'Excuse me, will you, just one moment? Shan't keep you.' With a whirl of her swivel chair she clip-clapped off to the rear of the office, vanished behind a screen.

At the next till, a customer was saying fretfully, 'You made up the interest to the thirty-first, but my point is, it should have been credited at the half-year stage and then added . . .'

Maisie felt a little sick. To take the strain off her knees, she supported herself on the counter-edge with her elbows and rested her forehead lightly against the glass screen; it was cool to her skin. Aching to close her eyes, she was afraid that if she did she would lose balance entirely and topple to the carpeted floor, arousing unwelcome attention. Blinking hard, she turned her head to stare at the branch entrance.

Nigel was standing near to it, his back to a poster-infested wall, arms folded across his chest, one impeccably trousered knee behind the other. The wave of his sandy hair glinted in the artificial light. Catching her eye, he freed a hand to salute her.

The cashier reappeared, passbook in hand. With a quick glance at the door she resettled herself, gave Maisie a wide smile, said brightly, 'Sorry for the delay.'

She began tapping keys on the contraption arranged at an angle next to her. The computer terminal? Some such device, Maisie recalled mistily, had been referred to grandly by Eric on various occasions when he came back from making an investment. Her six thousand pounds seemed to involve a lot of tapping. Finally the passbook slithered into a slot, stayed there a few moments while the girl stared intently at another part of the gadgetry which was just out of Maisie's view. When the book re-emerged, the girl slipped another cheque between the pages and shut it up. She passed it beneath the screen.

'There you go.'

'Thank you.' Maisie made a grab for it, missed, clawed again, scooped it towards her. The girl leaned forward.

'Now that your balance has dropped, so will the rate of interest, you know.'

'Beg pardon, dear?'

'Until the balance returns above five hundred, you'll be getting the lower rate.'

'I see. That's all right.' To Maisie, the information was gibberish. She just wanted to get away. 'Thank you for your help,' she said breathlessly, dimly aware of faces passing within a foot of her as she followed the rope handrail back to where Nigel was waiting. At her arrival he caught her by the arm.

'Okay, my love?'

'I've got the cheque.'

'Give it here, then, before it breaks your wrist. Sure you're feeling all right? The van's just outside. Don't want you making the place untidy, do we?'

'I'm fine.'

'That's my girl.' He examined the cheque. 'N. J. Murphy, six thousand pounds . . . and no pence. Good. We'll stop off at my bank, then I'll take you home and you can make yourself a nice cup of tea.'

'Then can I see Ouncey?'

'That,' Nigel said gravely, 'depends rather on Dave.'

'But surely—'

Steering her through the swing door, he led her back to the van. 'Cautious type, our Dave,' he explained, packing her inside. 'He may not feel like relinquishing his security until he . . . Well anyhow, Mrs Holwood, you've nothing to worry about, nothing whatsoever. The deal's all tied up, ends neatly sealed. A nice morning's work. You'll be glad, in the end, that you took our advice.'

Dave and Percy were consuming sandwiches. They had piled them on two of Maisie's plates from the kitchen, and were each supplied with hot tea in two of the yellow cups that she kept suspended from hooks under the wall-unit. Their jaws worked in unison. From the living-room door, Nigel appraised them.

'Sure you're perfectly comfortable?'

'Lunch break,' observed Percy, indicating the chiming clock on the mantelpiece.

'Since when did lunchtime start at eleven-thirty?'

'All a matter of personal taste, innit?'

'Taste? You haven't got any.' Helping Maisie to the chair at the table, Nigel winched her down into it. He turned to Dave. 'The security's banked, only we can't draw on it yet. Seeing that it's Mrs Holwood, though, we needn't let that hold the job up. You can make a start when you've had your nosh. Fed the dog yet?'

'Perce is seeing to it.'

'He mustn't be given the wrong food,' Maisie said urgently from her chair. 'There's a dish in the refrigerator with—'

'He'll have what Perce gives him.'

'Why can't I feed Ouncey myself?' She looked appealingly up at Nigel, who gazed back kindly.

'Leave it to Percy, my love, he's quite efficient.'

'Me? I don't know from nothing about animals. Why do I—'

'Stop arguing, Perce. You can cope.'

'He needs exercise, as well.' Maisie felt that she was talking in the middle of a nightmare, trying to get through to an audience of faceless, uncomprehending listeners. 'He'll get out of condition without it.'

Percy took a large gulp of tea. 'What am I, a craftsman or a bleeding vet?'

'Language, Perce.'

'Why can't it be left to me, Nigel? Percy doesn't want the worry of him. Just tell me where Ouncey is and I can—'

'Shut up, you old bag!' Dave shouted from the sofa.

Nigel's eyes closed briefly. 'See what I mean, Mrs Holwood? Dave's sensitive. Doesn't take a lot to get him all
upset. Right, Dave?'

The younger man bit broodingly into a white bread
sandwich, relaunched his jaws into rhythmic movements.

'And when he's edgy, of course, he's liable to do things
that . . . wouldn't occur to him otherwise. So what I suggest,
my love, is this.' Falling into his crouch position, Nigel
gazed benignly into her eyes. 'You let things ride for a
few days, just while the cheque's being cleared: after that,
maybe, you can take over again as head cook and bottle
washer, just as you were before. Nothing too upsetting in
that, is there?'

Maisie stared back in terror. *'Maybe?'*

'We have to keep our options open,' he pointed out
reasonably. 'Allow for the unexpected. As I said, Ouncey
represents collateral. Dave knows this. Which is why he's
jumpy.'

'You've got the money. What more do you want?'

'We've got a piece of paper,' Nigel corrected her patiently.
'Unless and until it's duly processed, we don't know what
obstacles might arise, do we? So we have to maintain our
cover. Once the cheque's cleared, we should be in a position
to restore the status quo. All else being equal.'

'And then I can have Ouncey back?'

He patted her knee. 'I see no reason why not.'

'You're quite sure he's all right? They've not—'

'Now don't you go imagining things, Mrs Holwood. No
call for that.'

'If I just knew he was safe and well . . .'

'Sit tight, my love, and leave everything to us. When
you're ready, lads. Back on the roof, get it all shipshape for
Mrs Holwood before the April showers decide to take a
hand.'

*

Shortly after four o'clock, Maisie was roused from a confused slumber by the stomping return into the room of Dave and Percy, brushing dust from their overalls into her tattered Axminster.

'Done all we can for now,' Dave said briefly to Nigel, who was pouring himself coffee from a pot he had made earlier in the afternoon.

'Much left?'

'Topping and tailing. Perce can see to it tomorrow.'

'Shocking state, it was,' Percy volunteered earnestly. 'All them March gales . . .'

'Just what I've been telling Mrs Holwood.' Nigel took delicate sips at his brew. 'Storm damage, wear and tear . . . it all mounts up. Carried out the work to specification, have you?'

'Decayed timbers stripped out,' recited Percy, who seemed to be having trouble controlling his mouth. 'Load-bearing rafters renewed as necessary: replacement felting and battens: re-slating to grade one standards. Ridge-capping to be done tomorrow, a.m. Weather permitting.'

'There you are, my love. Dave and Percy between them have done you proud. Virtually a new roof, should last a lifetime. And slap an immediate fifty per cent on the value of your property, into the bargain.'

Maisie looked dazedly from one to another. 'You've done all that in an afternoon?'

'Fast workers, my blokes,' Nigel informed her seriously, replacing his coffee cup tidily on the tray. 'Give them a few hours, in clement conditions, and there's no holding them. We'll be off, then, and leave you in peace.' At a leisurely pace he rose from the sofa where he had been leafing through Maisie's copy of the *Daily Monitor* when she dropped off to sleep. 'You'll be seeing Percy again tomorrow morning, for another hour or two. Meanwhile—'

'Is Ouncey all right? Has he been seen to?'

'Don't you go bothering yourself about him.'

'But I *am* bothered.' Maisie wept a little into her sleeve. 'I want to know he's being looked after.'

'What is it I was telling you, my love, before you had your nap?'

Maisie shook her head in an attempt to clear it. 'I don't remember . . .'

He tutted. 'There's nothing difficult about it,' he said reproachfully. 'All you have to promise is that you'll follow instructions and avoid saying anything of a negative nature about the quality of the repairs . . . get enough of that sort of talk, don't we lads, when it's not justified by the facts? Hurtful, we find it. Dents our professional pride.'

'I won't say anything. I've promised that.'

'Except how pleased you are with the job. If anybody should ask.'

'You can depend on me.'

'Good girl. And just as soon as we've cashed that cheque,' Nigel added, buttoning his jacket lazily and eyeing his coiffeur in Maisie's brass-framed mirror over the fireplace, 'you'll have Ouncey back to keep you company. In all probability.'

Maisie's held jolted on her neck. 'Can't you say for certain?'

'What's certain,' Nigel asked on a philosophical key, 'in this life? Who can guarantee the end result of any course of human conduct?' He smiled beatifically at his workforce. 'All we can do, us poor mortals, is labour assiduously and hope for the best. So, keep your pecker up, Mrs Holwood. We don't want any harm to come to the little fellow. With cooperation all round, I'm sure that can be avoided. Bye-bye for now, my love.'

CHAPTER 4

At a nearby table, an elderly woman was hunched over a sticky bun, applying butter to its perimeter with the intensity of a research biochemist examining a culture. Watching her, Anita felt a spasm of guilt that puzzled her vaguely.

The hair. It was the hair, she decided. Or rather, the relative lack of the commodity. The handful of grey, brittle strands that crawled about the old woman's scalp had put Anita subconsciously in mind of Auntie Maisie, whose crowning glory had undergone similar devaluation over the years; from there, only a low murmur had been required from her conscience to make itself heard. Too long had elapsed since her last visit. Three weeks. Getting on for four. She was guilty of neglect, and there was no excuse for it.

Other people seemed to manage. Other women, many of them older than she, held down full-time jobs while bringing up a family and having hobbies. And most of them, no doubt, with dependent relatives whom they called upon twice a week. If they could rise to the challenge, why not she?

Not everybody, of course, worked from eight-thirty to six in a salon, Monday to Friday, with half an hour for lunch and no personal transport. Her self-esteem revived a little. All things considered, she perhaps didn't do so badly. But today *was* Saturday. She ought to be able to find time and energy for things other than shopping. Lowering her copy of the *Informer* languidly to her knees, Anita sat back in her basket chair at the window of Ponsonby's Verandah Lounge and turned her attention to the High Street, which was fast acquiring its weekend mid-morning atmosphere of controlled frenzy. For a smallish and fairly undistinguished

town in the East Midlands, set in a belt of other smallish and
likewise unremarkable satellites of the main Birmingham/
Coventry conurbation, Barmston, she had often thought,
seemed to possess an animation factor well in excess of its
visible potential. On a Saturday, it positively hummed. Out
there, on the other side of Ponsonby's plate glass, useful and
rewarding things were waiting to be done by people just
like herself. What, she asked herself dejectedly, could they
possibly be, and why wasn't she out there doing them?

'Hi, Nita. Mind if I plonk myself here?'

An injection of pure dismay froze her bloodstream finally
in its course. Of all the faces in Britain, that of Selina Hodges
was the least welcome at this instant. It was all she could
do to bring herself to glance up.

'Hullo, Selly.' How had she come to connive in this
fatuous conspiracy of title-corruption? Because she lacked
the strength of mind to buck the trend, that was why. Yet
another minus-mark to go down on the record. 'No, help
yourself. I shan't be stopping long.'

'You won't?' Selina's bovine features sagged further in
disappointment. Claiming the opposite chair, she arranged
her Danish pastry and mammoth tumbler of orange juice
in tactical order on the glazed surface of the table, dumped
the tray at her feet and fixed Anita with a glare that
was half-applauding, half-accusatory. 'You should, you
know. You need the rest. You look awfully whacked. I
thought so yesterday. I was watching you, trying to work
miracles on old Mrs Ferguson's ghastly thatch, and I said
to Maureen—'

'I'm not ready for the health farm—yet.' Anita spoke
more brusquely than she had intended. The notion of being
studied while at work, and by Selina and Maureen of all
duos, was nearly enough to send her screaming out of the
building. 'Oddly enough,' she added, stuffing the *Informer*
back into her straw bag as a substitute gesture, 'I was

actually trying to relax when you came along. What wears
me out, I find, is small talk. The kind you have to keep up
with the customers. Don't you find that?'

'Gosh, you bet,' Selina returned, failing by a margin of
several miles to pick up the hint. 'Hard to think of anything
to say, isn't it, sometimes? I mean, if it's not package
holidays it's what their nephews are up to, and if it's not
their nephews it's their ingrowing toenails . . .'

'You seem to have better luck than me.' Anita picked up
her bill. 'All I get is politics . . . or else colitis. I must be
off. Got to look at shoes.'

'What kind are you after?' Selina was gripped instantly.
'There's that new place just opened, next to—'

'And after that I must look in on an aunt of mine.
Great-aunt, that is.'

Selina's eyes misted. 'Typical of you, Nita. Out on your
feet, and still thinking of others. She must be getting on a
bit?'

'In her eighties,' Anita said crisply. 'My mother was fond
of her. Just before she died, she asked me to keep an eye on
her if possible, so I . . . I do try.'

'That's great. Where does she live?'

'This barn of a house in Elm Chase. She ought to sell it,
move into a flat, but she won't. Although it's too big for her
and she's cut off from the neighbours, she insists on staying
there so that her dog can use the garden for exercise.'

'Oh, she's got a dog?'

'A Yorkie. About the size of a hedgehog, and nearly as
spiky. But she worships him. So long then, Sally. See you
Monday. Enjoy your snack.'

The bus took her as far as Pembroke Street, from where it
was a short walk to the Elm Chase junction. Now that she
had committed herself to a visit, Anita felt virtuous and less
exhausted. A chat with Auntie Maisie was always something

of a stimulus. Each time she called, she reminded herself that she ought to give herself a shot of it more often, for both their sakes.

Last time, her great-aunt had seemed in moderately good shape, despite a severe winter. But this was no excuse for the time gulf that had occurred since. In future, Anita vowed to herself, it would have to be at fortnightly intervals, no longer. Otherwise she was not keeping her word.

The front garden, she noticed on gaining the drive, looked if possible more unkempt than usual. Such shrubs as survived were becoming irretrievably entangled with the hotchpotch of trees that grew out of them, and the dying remnants of the few daffodils that had struggled through to daylight, lay sprawled across what had started out as asphalt but was now crumbling cinder, sprouting weed. On top of this, there was fresh disorder. Scattered near the porch were oddments of builders' materials: a bucket, a stiff brush with bent bristles, a pile of plastic imitation roofing slates of a peculiar grey-green. Frowning at them, Anita stepped through the obstruction and thumbed the doorbell, braced for the usual counter-tenor outburst from Ouncey. Greeted by silence, she frowned again.

If Auntie Maisie had taken the dog out, it was a rare occurrence. Normally she left him to pursue his own keep-fit regimen in the back garden, suitably enclosed with wire netting. Having waited, Anita rang again while preparing to return to the street: there had never been a delay before. Her great-aunt had once been in service, and the habit of prompt reaction to doorbells had stayed with her for life. On the point of walking away, Anita hesitated. The front door had quivered almost imperceptibly in its frame, although it remained shut. Stooping, she brought her mouth close to the letter-flap.

'Auntie? It's me—Anita. Are you there?'

The faintest of scuffing noises reached her. She began to

feel alarm. Had her great-aunt been taken ill? She might be crawling down the hall, fighting to reach and open the door. 'Auntie Maisie?' she bawled. 'Are you all right?'

The door opened suddenly, startling her. The sight of her only known relative, standing there as always in shapeless skirt and cardigan and open-toed casuals, was something of a relief; at the same time, Anita felt an obscure sense of disquiet. Auntie Maisie seemed to have been struck dumb. She just stood there, staring up with huge brown eyes, as if waiting to be told something. Anita summoned her widest smile.

'Have I called at a bad time? I thought you might not be well.'

'It's you, dear.'

Odder yet. If Anita had not known better, she might have been tempted to imagine that her great-aunt was not entirely certain of her visitor's identity ... or even that Anita's arrival was less than welcome. They had always got on together so well. Surely, within the space of less than a month, senility could not have struck with such blinding impact? Masking her trepidation, Anita said cheerfully, 'I've been meaning to call round for the past week. How are you, Auntie? How's the arthritis?'

'I'm all right, dear.'

Auntie Maisie's gaze slid past her to search the front garden. Anita glanced round as well. 'Are you expecting someone else?'

'No!' The reply sounded too quick, over-emphatic. As if aware of the fact, Auntie Maisie manipulated her face into the semblance of a hospitable expression and tugged at the door. 'Don't stand there. Come inside, out of the draught. Did you get the bus to the corner?'

'Same as always.' Stepping into the hall, Anita couldn't help noticing its state of comparative neglect. Dust had accumulated on the carved mahogany hatstand and

umbrella rack that had stood against the wall for as long
as she could recall, and the Wilton mats on the floorboards
were visibly unswept. Her great-aunt had always coped so
heroically with the housework. Was she now finding it
too much? 'I'm still pondering that car,' Anita added,
re-latching the door and accompanying the hunch-
shouldered small figure along to the 'sitting-room' at the
gaunt rear of the house. 'But it's no use unless I get a licence
. . . and I've not even plucked up courage to take lessons
yet. I wish I wasn't such a duffer at things.'

'Car?' Her great-aunt repeated the word with an air of
total abstraction.

'The one I was telling you about, last time. Belongs to
the brother of a colleague of mine at the salon. Fiesta. It's
still up for sale. But he's not going to hang on to it for ever,
is he, while I make up my mind? Point is, if I make him an
offer and then botch my driving test, I'll have wasted my
money. I suppose I could always resell it. Where's Ouncey?'

Pausing at the entrance, she peered around the living-
room for a glimpse of the tiny wriggling bundle that habitu-
ally threw itself at her ankles. 'In the kitchen,' Auntie Maisie
said indistinctly. 'Still, dear, it doesn't have to be that
particular car, does it? Plenty more to choose from. You can
take your pick.'

'Provided you've got the cash,' Anita said wryly. 'Not
sick, is he?'

'Who, dear?'

'Ouncey, of course. It's not like him to stay out of sight.'

'He's . . . having his lunch. Sit down, dear, and tell me
all about what you've been doing. Have a glass of sherry.
You'll find a bottle in the corner there. Glasses in the
sideboard.'

'I'll have one if you do.'

'All right, dear.'

Auntie Maisie had gone opaque again. Huddling herself

into the upright chair by the table, she had fastened her gaze upon the wreck of a garden beyond the french window, keeping it there with a fixity that suggested a bud-count of every twig in view. Eyeing her uneasily, Anita retrieved the sherry bottle from the floor and found a couple of dust-streaked wineglasses inside a cupboard of the side-board, a period piece in oak and brass which must have needed a block and tackle to get it into the room and would undoubtedly call for the modern version of such equipment when the time came to get it out again. Had that time come already? Anita's stomach pitched. Her great-aunt, she knew, was well turned eighty: conceivably within sight of ninety. If her mental faculties had started to go, nobody could have been surprised. Nobody except Anita herself, in whose eyes Auntie Maisie had become the living embodiment of a bygone and tougher epoch, a time when ordinary people were hewn in the bronze of stubbornness and smelted in the crucible of deprivation, giving them lasting resilience. But then, everyone was mortal. Sooner or later, even the Auntie Maisie's of this earth began to shed their armour. Telling herself this, Anita half-filled each wineglass with a fluid that looked and smelt not unlike the weedkiller her father had kept on an upper shelf of the garden shed when they were living in Staffordshire, and carried them across to the table.

'There you are, Auntie.' She rotated another chair into position. 'Still buying the treacly stuff from the supermarket, I notice.'

Auntie Maisie gave a start that was more of a shudder. 'What's that, dear?'

Anita tapped her wineglass. 'I think,' she said teasingly, 'they must have their own sugar plantations to produce the kind you like. Still, I must say, it goes down quite nicely after a week of the black coffee we get out of a robot at the salon . . . You're quite sure Ouncey's not ill?'

'He's eating his lunch, dear. I told you.'

'Normally that takes him about twenty-eight seconds. Then he yelps to come out, doesn't he?'

'He doesn't do that any more.' Auntie Maisie looked distractedly at the unoccupied bedding in the corner. After a brief silence she added, with manifest effort, 'Still keeping you busy, are they, at that place of yours?'

'Human hair seems to keep growing, come what may.' Seizing upon the topic as a route back to normality, Anita added, 'Like me to do something about yours, Auntie? Wash and set, same as last time?'

'You don't want to go to all that trouble.'

'It's no trouble.' Anita studied covertly the steely wisps that stuck out from her great-aunt's scalp like high altitude plant life clinging to rock. 'I can do it now, if you want.'

'Leave it till next time, shall we?'

'If you'd rather.' Anita felt rebuffed, and also baffled. What had become of Auntie Maisie's customary keen interest in everyday matters? 'Did I make a hash of it, the other week?'

'No, dear, of course not. It was very nice.'

Anita placed her sherry to one side. She had lost the taste for it, and the conversation. Inescapably, the dialogue was proving to be a struggle. Instead of being there, contributing to it, her great-aunt was elsewhere, watching other things, inexplicable things. Anita stood up.

'Well, Auntie, I think I'd better be off. I've a fair amount to do and you don't want me cluttering up the place. I expect you've plenty to occupy you, yourself.'

Auntie Maisie gave no hint that she had heard a syllable. Rising mechanically in Anita's wake, she followed her great-niece towards the door. 'Thank you, dear, for calling. Always pleased to see you.'

'I'll make it sooner, next time.' Anita hesitated. 'If you'd like me to.'

'As long as you're not too busy. Will you . . . be in time for the bus?'

'Auntie.' In the centre of the hall, Anita came to a halt. Her heartbeat had quickened a little. 'Has anything happened? You're not in trouble of some kind?'

'Whatever gives you that idea?'

'You'd tell me, if you were?'

'But I'm not, dear.'

'You don't seem *quite* yourself. And you say it's nothing to do with Ouncey? You haven't lost him?'

'Ouncey wouldn't go off. Not of his own accord.'

The old lady's posture had become rigid. And yet Anita thought she detected vibrancy in her great-aunt's diminutive frame: it was like seeing vapour escape from fissures in a volcano.

'Any dog can stray, though,' Anita pointed out gently. 'Or pick up a virus. Have you taken him to the vet?'

Auntie Maisie shook her head.

Puffing out her cheeks, Anita glanced towards the kitchen door. 'May I see him? Just to say hallo?'

'He doesn't like to be disturbed while he's eating.' Thin, bent fingers dabbed her towards the front door. 'Next time you call, he'll make it up to you.'

'Well . . . Enjoy the weekend.' Stepping reluctantly out into the porch, Anita turned to deliver a swift kiss to her great-aunt's forehead. The frigidity of the skin shocked her a little. 'And take care, won't you? Keep all the doors and windows bolted.' She nodded towards the pile of slates and other items strewn about the drive. 'Been having some work done?' she asked casually.

'Just a little patch-up job. The roof needed seeing to.'

'Did you have rain coming through?'

Auntie Maisie seemed not to hear. Stirring the synthetic slates with a foot, Anita added, 'You were lucky to find someone to do it. Who did you—'

'If you hurry now, dear, you'll be just in time for your bus. Nice to see you. Bye-bye for the present.'

Blowing a kiss, Auntie Maisie turned and retreated indoors, a dwarf retiring to her fortress. The door thumped behind her, awakening hollow echoes.

CHAPTER 5

'Dave? What's yours?'

'Pint of the best.'

'Why not? Seeing as we're in the money.'

'Not yet, we're not,' Nigel reminded them, gesturing to Frankie the barman.

'Good as. Only a few days to wait.' With an elbow on the bar, Percy watched Dave, who was studying with impassive countenance the assembled feminine clientele of the Merry Fiddler's saloon lounge. 'Thursday, you said, Nige?'

'Might be safer to leave it until Friday. No sense in rushing. What's another day, when there's a grand apiece in the pipeline?'

'May not be much to you,' Dave growled, fixing a heavily-inflated blonde in his sights, 'but for me and Perce it's different. Been a while since we pulled a good one.'

'That's right, Nige. And expenses don't melt away in the meantime, do they, Dave?'

'A grand apiece,' Nigel repeated, having exchanged confidential smiles with Frankie and apprized him of their requirements. 'For a day's labour, I don't call that chicken-feed.'

'Could be improved on.'

Nigel ignited a slender cigar. 'How come?' he inquired steadily, shaking out the match.

'Use your loaf.' Dave kept his eyes on the blonde while

he was speaking. She seemed to be with a bloke, but not inextricably so. 'The old bat's there by herself, right? No family, no lodgers. In a house the size of this place. So how does she do it?'

'Huh?' queried Percy.

'All them bills. Think about it. What's she using—Monopoly money?'

'She *did* have money,' Percy explained. 'What she's just donated to us.'

'Three grand? How long'd that last her?' Dave was assessing the physique of the blonde's companion, a thickset but rather short individual with a vaguely Indian or Pakistani look about him. From a short distance, he appeared to be of a peaceable, not to say timid disposition. 'She'd need capital. Real capital, I'm talking about. Ask me, all we've seen so far is the tip of the iceberg.'

'You could be right, Dave old son. Who knows? On the other hand,' Nigel continued smoothly, distributing the beer mugs as they arrived, 'it doesn't stand entirely to reason. Rates on that place would be sky-high, it's true, but she could be getting housing benefit. Even with her savings, she'd still be entitled.'

'Light, heating, food . . .'

'She probably lives in a couple of rooms. And feeds on tea and biscuits. You know what some of these old faggots are.'

'My mum does that.' Percy nodded sagely. 'Cornish wafers and Peekford's Assorted: all she ever buys. Seems to stay healthy on 'em. I was telling her, just the other—'

'We're not interested in your mum. It's the Holwood dame I'm talking about. I'm saying we've not . . .'

'Exploited?' suggested Nigel.

'Exploited the possibilities. Right. Three lousy grand in a building society? Red herring, that was.'

'You mean, she was just using it to fob us off?' Nigel

contemplated Dave calmly across the rim of his gin and tonic. 'So what if she did? We'd be fools to push our luck. Better a grand in the hand than a fortune in the slammer.'

'You saying there's a risk?' Dave made scoffing noises through the froth of his beer. 'Long as we've got her dog, what's the old witch going to do about it? Tell the neighbours?'

'It might not be the neighbours she chooses to approach.'

'The Fuzz? You're joking.' Wiping his mouth, Dave took note of the fact that the blonde had distanced herself from the Asian to watch a darts contest while appraising herself sidelong in a wall-mirror. 'Got her all stitched up, haven't we? If she bleats, her mutt gets it. She believes that. You could see it in her face.' Uprooting his gaze from the blonde, Dave replanted it on Nigel's blandly enigmatic features. 'What you having doubts for, all of a sudden? It was you had the idea in the first place.'

'I try to make it a rule, old son, never to milk an idea for more than it contains.'

'Yeah. That's why you've never struck it rich.' Dave glanced from Nigel to Percy, and back. 'You make me tired,' he observed. 'You're shown an opening, and all you want to do is chicken out. So, I'll go it alone.'

'Go what alone?' Nigel demanded.

'Exploiting the potential.'

'How do you propose to do that?'

'Go back there on Monday, put the screws on her.'

'You're insane. She'll—'

'And assuming I get results, they're all mine—okay?'

Nigel surveyed him for a moment; then shrugged. 'We can't stop you, Dave, if you've made up your mind. Just go easy, that's all.'

'Keep your shirt on. I know what I'm doing.'

'Don't overstep the mark, is my advice. You could land the three of us in trouble.'

'Don't have sleepless nights about it, Nigel old sport.' With a wink to Percy, Dave drained his tankard, replaced it on the bar counter and made adjustments to his leather jerkin. 'Meantime, seeing we've got prospects, how about a tenner on account?'

Having thought about it, Nigel produced a banknote which he handed over. 'Reducing your entitlement to nine hundred and ninety smackers—and don't you forget it.' With a glance across a shoulder, he lifted an eyebrow. 'I hope she turns out to be worth the exertion.'

Watching him head for the blonde, Percy released a lingering sigh. 'Headstrong,' he commented, with a blend of admiration and foreboding. 'That's Dave for you, in the proverbial nutshell. Reckon he's going to louse it up for us, Nige?'

The leader of the trio took a pull at his cigar. 'No,' he said presently. 'But he might make things awkward for himself.'

For most of the night, Maisie cried into the wing of her special armchair. She slept in it always. With the aid of the tablets which the doctor gave her for the arthritis, she could normally get through the hours of darkness with her heels on a footstool and Ouncey warm on her lap. He cramped her a little, but the price was a small one.

For the past few nights she would have been overjoyed to pay a price ninety times larger; but it had not been exacted. No somnolent weight had pinned her down, succouring her through the small hours. Each time she wept, Maisie still half-expected to feel the ministrations of a tiny cold nose on her cheek: its absence was more than she could take. The previous night, she had actually stumbled several times around the garden, calling to the dog in defiance of drizzling rain and a temperature close to freezing. Anita would have had something to say about that.

Desolate thoughts of her great-niece occupied her for a while. She had, she knew, been less than welcoming that morning. Anita would never visit her again.

But what choice had she had?

You mention this to a living soul, the dog gets it. All right?

Given the chance, Nigel would have stuck up for her: Maisie felt convinced of that. Against Dave, though, he was obviously powerless. He couldn't even know where Ouncey was being kept, otherwise he would have told her. Anyone who looked as much like her Billy as Nigel did must have a decent side to him. As for that Percy . . .

Just a stooge, he was. Dave was the real menace. Dave, who had Ouncey.

Thrusting herself laboriously upright, Maisie sat gasping for a few moments while the thumbscrews clamped to her joints loosened themselves marginally, enabling her in the end to stand, totter across to the door. Reaching the kitchen, she stood looking vacantly at the ancient equipment. The gas cooker with its wobbly plate-rack. The yellowing refrigerator. The porcelain sink with its scratched-in grime that only dousings of bleach could shift.

Why had she come out here? To make tea: that was it. She didn't want tea, but it was an occupation. Ordinarily, Ouncey would have been sharing it with her. The tears started to flow again.

Admonishing herself to be less stupid, Maisie advanced sternly to the sink and filled the kettle.

Mention this to a living soul . . .

Inspiration smote Maisie. In her excitement she nearly dropped the kettle. She needn't tell anyone . . . but she could report Ouncey missing. That would get the authorities active on her behalf, without breaking her pledge. A clever compromise. If she merely knew that something was being done, some action undertaken . . .

Planting the half-filled kettle on the drainer, she made

with laborious haste for the telephone in the hall. With the receiver clutched in her hand she paused, debating what to dial. Should it be 999? It was, after all, an emergency. Ouncey might not be eating. That would affect his health. Hauling the local phone book painfully from its nest of outdated volumes, she looked up Police.

Several numbers were given. Choosing that which sounded nearest, she dialled it and waited, trembling in the silent chill of the hall, her heart hammering. When a female voice answered, Maisie had to clear her throat twice before words would emerge.

'I want to report a dog missing.'

The request was met by a brief silence. 'Is it urgent, madam? Or could you phone us after daybreak?'

'I'd sooner tell you now, please,' Maisie said firmly.

'Hold the line.' The voice was heavily resigned. Waiting, Maisie rehearsed her opening remarks, secure in the expectation of a deep, fatherly vocal recipient of the kind to which she had been conditioned as a girl—'If you're ever in trouble of any sort, Maisie, go and ask a policeman'—the kind she had encountered on the traumatic occasion of Billy's accident when everyone had been so comforting. True, they had never traced the hit-and-run motor cyclist who eye-witnesses vouched had been responsible for knocking him down; but you could hardly blame the police for that. They had done their level best. And the sympathy she had received, especially when . . .

'Valuable dog, is it, madam? Just lost him?'

'He's been gone three days,' she quavered. All her prepared approaches were knocked out of her mind. Instead of the fatherly voice, it sounded more like one belonging to a junior pupil at the Wellington Avenue Comprehensive . . . and none too nicely spoken a sample, at that. Maisie had several times overheard a cross-section of them on their way out from school, when she was walking Ouncey. What was

this one doing in the police force? Maisie felt confused. She
could think of nothing more to say.

'Three days.' The words were uttered without inflexion.
Another short pause. 'Any idea, madam, what time it is at
the moment?'

Maisie looked stupidly about her. There was no clock in
the hall. Her watch lay on the living-room table. 'I don't
. . . I'm not . . .'

'It's half past one in the morning.'

'Is it? I see.'

'D'you *want* to give us the details now? Or call in the
morning?'

'I thought, perhaps—'

'Only I'm *rather* busy, you see, with some hooligans
they've just landed on me. Can you give us a bell after nine?'

Maisie looked helplessly down at the receiver.

'Or you could call in. There'll be someone here to—'

Maisie hung up.

For a few moments she stood in a state of mental and
physical paralysis. Moonglow filtered through the leaded
lights of the front door's upper half, spread itself over the
mat. From the living-room, the chiming clock on the mantelpiece sounded the half-hour.

Finally she got herself on the move again. Back inside the
kitchen, she finished the job of kettle-filling, connecting plug
to socket. Inserting a teabag into the pot, she stood waiting
for the water to boil. Fifteen minutes later, she found that
she had forgotten to switch on the power.

'Why don't you get yourself a car?' demanded the blonde
irritably. 'Be a sight more comfy.'

'What's wrong with the van?'

'What's right with it?' Slithering clear of him, she made
adjustments to her skirt and reached across the floor of the
loading area for her sweater. 'Stinks of cement dust, and I

reckon I've been lying on the end of a shovel. You work for a builder?'

'I'm a works contractor,' Dave corrected her. In the near-darkness of the van's interior, her movements were maddeningly obscured. 'More space in here than you'll get in a saloon. If you're crazy for a car, though, I'll buy a car.'

'Oh, don't go to any trouble on my account.' Amending her attitude on reflection, the blonde added, 'Would you though, seriously? You're a funny one, Dave. We've only just met.'

'Why waste time?'

'A girl don't like to be rushed.' She pulled the sweater on with dignity. 'You could flog this old heap,' she suggested, reclaiming her leather coat, 'and swap it for one of them four-wheel-drive jobs. They're fabulous.'

'May do that.'

'They don't come cheap.'

'I've cash coming to me.'

'From a job?'

'That's it. A job.'

'Must've been a big 'un, if you're thinking about a Ranger.'

'Not as big,' Dave said significantly, 'as the one coming up Monday. Could be a cracker.'

'How d'you mean, *could* be?'

'Depends.'

'If they want it done, you mean? If they can afford it?'

'Near enough.' Dave emitted a snort that passed as laughter. 'All a question of the available finance.'

'How much are we talking about?'

'This job I've just done . . .' Dave paused briefly. 'It'll net me a grand.'

'No kidding?'

'Compared with Monday, though, that could turn out to be peanuts.'

'Bloomin' heck.' The blonde was impressed. 'Yes, but how long's it going to take you? Six months?'

Dave shook his head. 'If it comes off, it'll be quick. In my trade, we don't mess about.'

Zipping up the leather coat, she peered at his outline suspiciously. 'Don't sound much like construction work, to me. Sure it's nothing crooked?'

'Do us a favour. Do I look like that sort of bloke?'

'You don't look like any sort of bloke to me. Can't even see you.'

'We'll meet up again, then, in daylight,' he said promptly. 'Call round for you, tomorrow afternoon?'

'I'll think about it.'

'Don't think too hard. Your dad runs the Fiddler, that right? So I can pick you up there. Let's have your name.'

'Just ask for Bella.' Struggling to her knees, she patted her hair back into formation. 'If I'm not down in one of the bars, they'll send up for me. If I'm there, and if I feel like it, I might come down . . . if I'm not too busy.'

'Tomorrow's Sunday,' Dave told her coolly. 'You won't be busy.'

CHAPTER 6

Anita woke with an urge to talk.

In the normal way, she was content to steer clear of her neighbours. They were not an inspiring bunch. Immediately next to her on the second-floor landing dwelt an embittered divorcee in her middle years with a seemingly unquenchable thirst for discussing men and their shortcomings with any available female: Anita had long ago written her off. On the floor above, the elderly male occupant of what was

grandiosely described as The Penthouse had a habit of
pacing across his woodblock flooring in hobnailed boots at
inconsiderate moments, but was otherwise harmless, and
devoid of conversational flair. The remaining tenants of the
property, one of the handful in the district still rented out,
arrived and departed like wraiths, occasionally bumping
into each other at the main entrance or standing aside with
exaggerated courtesy on the stairs. Anita knew most of them
by sight. One or two looked interesting, but opportunities
for developing acquaintance were rare to the point of non-
existence, and on the whole it had suited her to keep things
that way.

Until now. Eight-fifteen on a Sunday morning, and she
had no one to confide in. She couldn't ring Fiona, her best
friend at the salon, because Fiona was away for the weekend;
cruising the Norfolk Broads, of all wind-blistered places,
with a new boyfriend who fancied himself as a deckhand.
None of Anita's other colleagues was on her waveband or
anywhere in sight of it. It was at times like this, she reminded
herself ruefully, that a self-contained lifestyle was apt to
backfire on one. Somebody in the family would have been
useful. Other people had families. How come she had been
deprived of her share, so early?

Emerging restlessly from her apartment door, Anita tiptoed along the landing to the adjacent oblong of varnished
veneer that concealed the refuge of the man-hating Ms.
Trubshaw and stood eyeing it speculatively. It was a
measure of her need, she thought gloomily, that she was
prepared even to contemplate subjection to a diatribe on
the subject of male villainy, in return for some dialogue
on other matters . . . if the exchange could somehow be
channelled along those lines. Her fingertip was actually on
the bellpush when a pounding of footsteps on the staircase
below froze her muscle. She glanced round.

Into sight came a tousled head. 'Hi,' said the mouth

belonging to it. 'You wouldn't happen to have any spare milk?'

'I could probably manage a cupful. Are you out?'

'Mine's gone off. Left it out of the fridge overnight. And the milkman's been and gone.'

'Let's take a look.' Anita walked back to her own door, leaving him to follow. Instead of waiting at the flat entrance, as she had assumed he would, he tailed her through to the kitchen where he stood relaxed, arms hugging his chest, while she sought and found a milk carton, one-third full, that had been open since Tuesday. 'Should still be drinkable,' she said, handing it to him. 'It keeps quite well, as a rule. Or I've got Long Life. Or a sachet of half-cream?'

Pouring a taster on the back of his hand, he sampled it. 'This'll do fine. Can I pay you for it?'

'Yes.' She shut the refrigerator door. 'You can give me a word of advice.'

When she turned, he was regarding her with whimsicality mixed with wariness. 'You want *me* to offer *you* advice?'

'Why? Do you charge for it, normally?'

The extent of her own pertness took her by surprise. She sensed, however, that he wasn't the type to take offence. Besides, they were not total strangers. In recent weeks they had met several times in the entrance lobby, helping themselves to personal mail from the communal table; and just a few days ago he had helped her upstairs with a bathroom wall-cabinet in which she had invested on impulse. By Highland House standards, they were practically old buddies.

'If I did,' he replied thoughtfully, resealing the milk carton, 'my rates would have to be pretty low. Mind you, it would depend partly on the category. In the field of emotional stress, I do quite a good line in—'

'Nothing like that. Well, emotion does come into it, I suppose, after a fashion. I'm worried about an aunt of mine.'

'Aunts. None too well up, I'm afraid, in that particular breed. This is one you're especially addicted to, I take it?'

'She's my great-aunt, actually. The only one I've got. Which is why I'm concerned.'

He leaned against the doorpost. 'Because she's pushing on in years?'

'Partly. And partly because I'm afraid she might possibly be getting a bit . . . you know . . .'

'Less alert,' he suggested, 'than she used to be?'

'That's a nice way of putting it. Look, I'm keeping you,' she added as he made a movement. 'You're gasping for coffee. Forget I mentioned it.'

'No, really.' Depositing the milk carton on top of the refrigerator, he advanced to rest a lean hip against a work-top, refolding his arms like an examining magistrate. His hair, she noted, was inches too long and exceedingly untidy. Clean, though, and a good shade. Copper-brown, with a coarse texture that would make it easy to handle. Her fingers itched to get at it. Diverting them to her own raven tracery, which itself was badly in need of a wash, she steered it absently into a fresh course behind each ear while letting him talk on. 'I don't mind having a bash. You're upset. I'm available. Why don't we give it a spin, see what flies off?'

'I wouldn't say I was upset, exactly.' Anita took stock of herself. 'Unsettled. Up to now, you see, she's seemed quite capable of looking after herself, but when I called on her yesterday . . .'

'She'd slipped a bit?'

'Didn't seem to be with me. Normally she's so interested, so . . . responsive.'

'Everyone has off-days.'

'Not my Auntie Maisie. Never before, to my knowledge. Then there was her dog.'

'He off-colour, too?'

'That's the point, I've no idea. There was no sign of him.'

The face of the young man cleared. 'There's your answer. The hound's not well and she's out of her skull, fretting over it.'

'She'd have told me. But no, every time I asked, she clammed up.'

He pondered. 'Afraid you'd insist on whisking it off to the vet?'

'She's never minded Ouncey seeing the vet. If he so much as choked on his petmeal, she'd rush him off. Auntie Maisie has no inhibitions in that direction, I can assure you.'

'But yesterday she was inhibition itself?'

'She made me feel I was intruding. That's not like her. Apart from which, she looked wretched and . . . I don't know. Frightened.'

Her visitor glanced up from a study of the kitchen floor. *'Frightened?'*

'That's the impression I had.'

Silence took over briefly. 'What sort of a dog is it?'

'Yorkie. The kind you can stuff into a handbag, and exercise by sending it twice up the stairs and back. He suits Auntie Maisie, and she's batty about him.'

'Is he a yapper?'

Anita grimaced. 'He can make his presence felt.'

'I was wondering whether one of the neighbours . . .'

'Oh, I'm sure it's nothing like that. Who'd be so unkind? Anyhow, there again she'd have been only too eager to confide in me. But all she seemed to want to do was get me out of the house. Why?'

'If you really want my advice,' the young man said self-deprecatingly, after a moment's thought, 'I'd buzz back there and ask her.'

'She might think it a bid odd. I was only there yesterday morning.'

The eyebrows of her counsellor shot up. 'There's a statutory limitation on your visits?'

'Of course not, but . . .'

'You don't want her to feel that you're nosing into her affairs? I wouldn't let that stop you. If she's in trouble, she might be darn glad of some help. Maybe she didn't like to ask.'

'That's possible.'

'Obviously you feel some responsibility for her. So, until you clear your mind, you're not going to grab much sleep. Get back there and demand pointblank to be shown Yorkie, or else.' The young man paused. 'Does that,' he inquired solemnly, raising the carton, 'pay for the milk ration?'

'Handsomely.' She followed him to the vestibule door, her mind active. 'You've pointed me in the right direction, I think—thanks a lot.'

'My pleasure. I'm a fount of good sense and logic . . . when it's not myself I'm trying to guide. How does this thing open? Oh, I get it. Well, see you around. Good luck with Auntie Maisie.'

'I'll let you know,' she called over the landing balustrade, 'anything I find out.'

'Do that. I'll be interested.'

For lunch, Maisie poached herself an egg at eleven-fifteen and then burned the toast she was to have had it on, so she ate it unaccompanied. Or as much of it as she could stomach, which was less than half. Food choked her. The remaining overcooked portion she placed carefully inside the refrigerator for Ouncey: he enjoyed an egg, cooked or raw, and by this time tomorrow . . .

She tried not to dwell on the possibility. Returning to the living-room, she stood looking around blankly, wondering how to get through the rest of the day. If her limbs had ached less, she would have roamed the streets for another hour, hoping by some miracle to catch sight of Ouncey being held captive in some garden or hear his unmistakable voice from inside a house. By her reasoning, it was perfectly feasible that Dave lived in the area. Perhaps quite near at hand. If not, how had he spirited Ouncey away so effectively during the half-hour that she and Nigel had been absent, withdrawing the money?

He could have stowed the dog in Nigel's car, which had been left parked by the porch while they drove into town in the van. But in that case, Ouncey would have protested vocally and she would have heard him on their return.

Unless . . .

Maisie closed down her mind. There were certain eventualities that were best left unconsidered. Think positively, she adjured herself. Wherever he was at this moment, Ouncey needed her. He might be starving. He could be wet and cold and miserable, pining for home. His rescue was up to her: there was nobody else.

'Mummy's coming, darling,' she said aloud, turning with painful decisiveness to fetch her outdoor shoes from the hall. Aches or no aches, she would push herself forth once more, cover a few more streets. The miracle could still occur.

As she crammed her right foot into its shoe, the doorbell blurted.

Her heart gave a skip. No one ever called on a Sunday. It must be Dave, seized by remorse, returning Ouncey. Or Nigel, who was on her side. Perhaps he had prevailed upon his associate to relent in advance of whatever deadline had been set. Breathlessly she hobbled to the door, unchained it, dragged it back.

For an idiotic moment the figure standing in the porch was meaningless to her. If it had been the Queen in person, Maisie's mouth would have remained no wider agape. Even when she spoke, the caller sounded unfamiliar, putting a question that made no particular sense.

'Off out, Auntie? I thought you'd be getting your lunch.'

'I've had my lunch,' Maisie replied with dignity. She took

a breath. The crushing disappointment had left her short of wind. Then, with the dregs of her resources, she mustered elements of a smile. 'You're soon back, dear. Did you leave something here yesterday?'

'No, no. I just came along to see that you're all right.' Anita, who was wearing a different get-up—short suede jacket over flared skirt, above knee-high boots—sounded a little breathless herself. Maybe the damp weather was to blame. 'You didn't seem quite yourself yesterday, Auntie, I thought. So I decided to call back. Sorry if you were just leaving. Are you making for the bus?'

'No, dear. Just off for a stroll.' Defensively she added, 'I had my meal early, you see, so as not to waste the afternoon. I do like my exercise.'

'Very good for you.' Anita pumped approval into her voice, but she was perplexed. Auntie Maisie's lifelong aversion to outdoor physical activity was faithfully documented in what she had seen of the family chronicles: had the old lady suddenly changed her outlook? And would she go without taking Ouncey? Anita studied her with increased suspicion. She didn't look good. Her face was a poor colour and her eyes were off-focus. For a few moments the two of them stood irresolute, until finally, reaching a decision, Anita put gentle pressure on her great-aunt's left elbow and steered her gently back along the hall towards the living-room. 'You're leaving Ouncey at home? I'd have thought he'd enjoy a breath of air.'

'Ouncey had a walk this morning.' Submitting limply to her great niece's pilotage, Maisie returned to her armchair, sat in it with her feet together, her gloves clasped in her lap.

'He's feeling better, then?'

'Better?' Maisie peered up vacantly.

'He didn't seem inclined to show himself yesterday. I wondered if he was out of sorts.'

'Ouncey's fine, dear. You've no need to worry.'

'But I'd love to see him. I've brought him a chewstick. Look.' Producing it from her jacket pocket, Anita held it up. 'Can I give it to him?'

'Thank you very much, dear. I'll see that he has it.'

'Auntie . . .' Sinking to her knees, Anita confronted her relative. 'You're holding out on me. He's not well, is he?'

'Whatever makes you think that? He's in the kitchen, asleep inside his—'

'Then why can't I see him?'

With dismay, she observed the tightening of her great-aunt's mouth. It occurred seldom, but when it did, as she knew from experience, there was no headway to be made. 'Ouncey's tired,' Maisie said firmly. 'The vet gave him some tablets for his coat, and they make him sleepy. He'll enjoy the chewstick, dear, when I give it to him later. Very thoughtful of you. Would you like a cup of tea before you go?'

'No, thanks, Auntie. I must get back.' Rising, Anita stood looking down at the small, solitary figure in the armchair. 'So, everything's terrific? No problems?'

'Getting along nicely, dear, thank you.'

'That's good.' Anita thrashed her brain for something else to say. 'I don't want tea,' she added in desperation, 'but I'm a bit dry—I could do with a sip of water.'

She waited tensely. Auntie Maisie, she thought, was unlikely to fall for such a ploy. To her amazement, the old lady made no move to labour to her feet, head her off. Her tale about Ouncey and the kitchen seemed to have slipped her mind. 'Help yourself, dear, from the tap. The cold one is on the left.'

Anita let herself swiftly into the kitchen. Its condition brought her momentarily to a standstill: never had she seen it so neglected. Used crockery and utensils were piled on drainer and worktop; on the cooker, a saucepan had boiled over and its contents left to congeal. Scarves and cardigans littered the unswept floor. A number of stale odours hung in the air. Of Ouncey there was no sign.

She called to him softly, without a response. Opening the larder door, she investigated it thoroughly, moving aside old shopping baskets and biscuit tins to explore the inner recesses. Emerging, she stood pondering, then took a tumbler from its shelf, half-filled it from the cold tap, returned with it to the living-room. Auntie Maisie was where she had left her, compact in the centre of the armchair, gazing vaguely at the opposite wall.

'Ouncey's not there, Auntie.'

To her horror, the old lady collapsed in a fit of sobbing. Her fists beat a feeble tattoo on the cushions. Crouching beside her, Anita flung a protective arm across her shoulders.

'Auntie, don't cry. Did he stray? Tell me all about it.'

She could feel her relative's bone structure through the meagre flesh. 'If Ouncey's lost,' she went on urgently, 'there's something we can do about it . . . provided you tell me what happened. Dry your eyes.' Finding a tissue, she pressed it into Auntie Maisie's palm, now unclenched and lying flaccidly on the upholstery.

Conveying the tissue to her right eye, Auntie Maisie tried to say something. Anita leaned closer to listen. As well as she could make out, her great-aunt was mumbling about someone called Michael, or possibly Nigel. 'Someone who took Ouncey out for you?' she asked. 'Lost him, did he? And you don't want to land him in trouble with his parents? Is that it?'

Maisie shook her head. After a sniff or two she returned the tissue, then sat in a silent slump, her forehead against Anita's upper arm. Presently, releasing herself with care, Anita offered her the tumbler. Maisie took a diminutive sip, handed it back.

'I can't tell you, dear.'

'Why ever not?'

'If I do, I shan't get Ouncey back.'

Anita stared. 'Auntie, you'll have to be more explicit. You mean someone's keeping him? Won't let him go?'

Maisie was silent.

'Got you scared, haven't they? Made threats? Who is it, and what are they after? Are they holding Ouncey to ransom?'

Still her great-aunt said nothing. Anita beat the air in frustration. 'If it's local youngsters, you know, we can certainly do something. The police—'

'Not the police, dear. We mustn't.'

'You've been warned not to contact them? That's quite usual, Auntie, but you must. They'll help. They can—'

'I'm not doing anything to hurt Ouncey.'

'The police know how to handle these things. If you don't call them in, you'll be ill with worry and then what will Ouncey do?'

'Let me deal with this, dear. I know what I'm doing.'

Anita walked agitatedly to the french window and back. 'You may know, but I certainly don't. Who's this Michael, or Nigel?'

Her great-aunt's mouth closed in an obstinate formation. Anita sat next to her on the edge of the chair. 'Tell me something, Auntie. Does this have any connection with that roofing job you had done?'

'I don't quite understand . . .'

'Were they cowboys? How much did they charge you for the work?'

'Nothing that I couldn't afford, dear. I paid by cheque.'

'Yes, but was it reasonable?' Anita waited a moment. 'Are we in time to get it stopped?'

'Stopped?'

'The cheque. If they've grossly overcharged—'

'We mustn't do anything like that, dear.'

'Otherwise you won't get Ouncey back? I knew it,' Anita said grimly. You've paid by cheque, and they're waiting for it to be cleared before . . .' She felt a tiny, convulsive movement of her great-aunt's body, and sprang up. 'I'm going to put a call through to the police. You need help, Auntie. These men have got to learn—'

With a sudden outburst of energy, Auntie Maisie propelled herself off the armchair. 'You're very kind, Anita, and I know you mean well, but I've given my word. For Ouncey's sake . . . He'll be here tomorrow, I expect.'

'Ouncey will?'

'Or Tuesday. They promised.'

'Who's bringing him? Michael?'

'Nigel, dear. The polite one. No, not him. The other one, I think. The one who's got Ouncey.'

'What's *his* name?'

'So you see, I mustn't say or do anything in the meantime. You do understand, don't you?'

Anita gazed at her in despair. 'I think I understand perfectly. They've got you right where they want you— eating out of their dirty hands. Look, Auntie. They won't *know* if you've gone to the police. They can't possibly. They've just scared you into thinking they will. So why don't we set a trap for them? The police—'

'No, dear. A promise is a promise.'

Anita hissed through her teeth. 'Mum always said how stubborn you were. But I might take after you, Auntie, for all you know. What if I decide to call the police anyway, after I leave here?'

Auntie Maisie peered up at her. 'You wouldn't do that, dear? You wouldn't put Ouncey in danger?'

Putting out a hand, Anita rumpled what remained of her great-aunt's hair. 'All right,' she said wearily. 'We'll give it until tomorrow evening. If Ouncey's not back by then, I'm reporting the matter. Agreed?'

Auntie Maisie bit her lip. 'I wish you wouldn't. I'm afraid that Dave . . .'

Her voice slurred away.

Anita said alertly, 'Dave? Is he the dognapper?'

The old lady returned silently to her armchair. Hurrying in pursuit, Anita helped her down into it, plumped the cushions, lifted her relative's thin legs on to the footstool. 'We'll say no more about it for the moment. I want you to sit there and relax while I make a nice pot of tea for both of us. Tea and toast. You don't look to me as if you've eaten properly for days.'

'Thank you, dear.' Maisie's head was starting to nod. 'You're very thoughtful. Just like your mother.'

'Have a doze. I shan't be long.'

Anita returned softly to the hall. The telephone, stained and dust-clogged, stood on its three-legged occasional table against the wall: moving towards it, she stretched out a hand. Her fingers hovered above the instrument. Presently, with a small impatient shake of the head, she withdrew them and returned to the kitchen. Putting water on to boil, she set to work on the chaos surrounding her.

CHAPTER 7

Steve Walsh fell out of mid-afternoon slumber with the sensation that something had disturbed him. The Sunday newspapers, he observed, had slid from his legs to the floor. As he was retrieving them, the doorbell resonated through the flat.

Mystery solved. Swinging long legs lazily to the carpet, he impelled himself with an effortful 'Woof' out of his chair and through to the vestibule, fingering hair out of his eyes.

The girl standing outside was smiling, though not with
her eyes, which were anxious. Steve grinned back blearily.
'Hi. Called for the empty carton?'

'Thought I'd make you a present of that.' Anita hesitated.
'I've come at a lousy time, I know. Three o'clock on a
Sunday—'

'On the contrary. You've rescued me from latent liver
damage.' He held the door hospitably back. 'Step right in.
If it's a cupful of sugar or an egg . . .'

'I don't want anything. Except more advice.'

'Blimey.' Steve scratched at his hair. 'I'll have to think
seriously about formulating a scale of fees. The great-aunt,
again?'

With a nod, she stepped past him towards the living-room
door. Placing a friendly palm against her shoulderblades,
he eased her through to the one sizeable area of his bachelor
apartment, wondering whether he was being taken for a
sucker. She might simply be lonely. But so what? If things
got out of hand he could readily call a halt, and she did look
genuinely worried. 'I'm flattered,' he told her, clearing
newsprint from the spare armchair, 'but mystified. There
must be people better qualified than me you could ask.'

'You're available,' she replied with candour, ignoring the
armchair as she turned to face him. 'Also, you gave me the
right tip this morning . . . so I'm hoping you can do it
again.'

'I'll try. Did you go back and see her?'

Anita nodded. 'It's what I was afraid of. She's in serious
trouble.'

'Let's hear about it.'

They both sat. While Anita was telling him, he unobtrus-
ively took stock of her. Allowing for a degree of dishevel-
ment —she looked as if she had been running—he perceived
quality in her personality, although in conventional looks
she would not, in his estimation, have moved mountains or

sunk armadas. For all that, he rather enjoyed the sight of her. Something in her movements, the way she held her head, glanced across at him with damson eyes set in a pale, thinly oval face, appealed keenly to his taste. Hitherto, meeting her briefly in the main lobby or on the stairs, he had assessed her as harmless but dull. Another snap judgement. Avoid them in future, he told himself, wondering what she thought of him.

'So I left her there, asleep,' she was saying, 'and made sure all the locks and things were fastened before I came away, meaning to go straight to the police station and report it. Only, before I got there I had second thoughts . . .'

'Why was that?'

'Because I'm not sure about the exact situation. Auntie Maisie was trying hard not to blab too much, but she's so naïve . . . She couldn't help letting one or two things slip. Even so, I'm rather in the dark. How much of a hold have these men got over her?'

'Good question.'

'I mean, could they have some means of knowing if I contacted the police?'

'I don't see you've much option. Obviously they've got to be called in.'

'Even if it led to Ouncey being . . .?'

'Especially if it led to that.'

'You're right,' she admitted, after a moment's thought. 'I'd feel like an assassin, but . . . No alternative, is there?'

'Afraid not. Want to ring from here?'

'I think I'd sooner speak to somebody in person. I'll call round at the station now, then get back to the house and see that she's all right. I don't want to leave her too long. Before coming away I slipped one of her sleeping pills into her tea, but it may not have a lasting effect. I think she normally takes a couple.'

Steve sprang up. 'My buggy's outside. I'll take you.'

'Oh, I couldn't dream of putting you to—'

'No need to dream. This is reality I'm offering.' Grabbing his jacket from a magazine stand, he zipped himself into it. 'Ready? Or could you use a drink first?'

'I could, but there's no time.' Accepting his hand, she let herself be hauled upright. 'It's over an hour already since I left her. The Sunday buses don't exactly jostle each other off the road. Look, I can't say how grateful I am. I don't even know your name.'

They got acquainted on the way downstairs. 'I'm away quite a bit,' Steve informed her, wresting the car keys from a hip pocket. 'Apart from you, there's hardly an occupant of this place I've swapped ten words with since I moved in. Not that I mind. Anti-social, that's me.'

'You don't give that impression. What's your job?'

'Travel writer. Heard of *Offshore*? It's a monthly.'

'I've seen it on the bookstands. Sounds fun.'

'It is fun. I can't deny it. I really do get to exotic places, live the life of Riley, all at my employer's expense. It's not work, it's recreation. People are nice to me. Hotel staff fawn and genuflect. I'm the luckiest cuss on any payroll.'

She laughed as they reached the street. 'That's refreshing to hear. Most people are full of the hidden drawbacks in their work. I tend to be, myself.'

'So now it's my turn to ask . . .?'

'Hair stylist,' she said briefly, rounding the car to its nearside. 'And I know, yes, I'm no advertisement for my profession and right now I don't care. I've too much on my mind.'

'Your hair looks great to me. Stop worrying. We'll have Great-Aunt Maisie in the caring hands of the constabulary before you can say . . . crime prevention. Hop in.'

The detective-sergeant to whom they eventually gained access at the police station took an immediate and serious interest. 'We'll call round,' he pledged, 'and have a quiet word with the old lady. She's lucid, I take it? Got her wits about her?'

'Except,' Anita said wryly, 'when it comes to cowboy builders. They seem to have fooled her completely.'

'You need to see how it's done,' remarked Sergeant Frank Bennett, finalizing the note he was scrawling on a pad. 'Some of these villains, I tell you, they could smooth-talk a City bank into coughing up a million-quid loan, without security. In the case of a single, elderly person . . .'

He sat shaking his head. 'Anyhow, Miss Blythe, you've done the right thing in coming to us. My suggestion now is that you get directly back to your aunt, see she's all right, if possible wait there with her until I or one of my colleagues can get along to interview her, find out precisely what's been happening. You've got transport?'

'Thanks to my friend here.'

'We'll see you again shortly, then. *Should* there be any approach from one of these bastards while you're around, stall him. But I doubt if you'll have that problem. They much prefer to swoop when their victims are alone. If you'll pardon the statement of the obvious.'

'Decent bloke,' Steve commented as they got back into the car. 'Hope he doesn't keep you waiting too long. Like me to stop on with you?'

'You've done enough as it is.'

'I think I should, though. Until the cops arrive.'

'All right. Thanks. I'll dish up a meal for the three of us. I think I spotted a tin of pilchards when I was tidying the kitchen.'

'That's too much for any man to withstand.' Steve accelerated off. 'In the normal way, I suppose, Auntie Maisie cooks for herself? Or does she have Meals on Wheels?'

Despite her anxiety, Anita had to chuckle. 'She'd be far more likely to volunteer for taking them round to other people. Youngsters of eighty, I mean. The fact that she's getting on a bit herself never seems to dawn on her.'

'An independent lady. One of the originals.'

'They don't seem to come like it any more.' Anita was silent for a while. 'Got any ancient relatives, Steve, yourself?'

He scowled. 'There's rumoured to be a cousin of sorts in Fife, but I've never met her. We're not much of a tribe. Just me, my parents—they run a betting shop on the South Coast, would you believe?—and my sister, who's five years older than me, and respectably wed, and living in Berkshire. Do your parents live locally?'

'My mother's dead.'

'Sorry. And your dad?'

'He ran off with a chiropodist when I was eight. I don't even know if he's still alive. He's never been in touch.'

Steve flipped her a glance. 'So you and Great-Aunt Maisie are kind of survivors?'

'Both clinging on for dear life. She's always insisted I take after my mother—and her. If so, I'm flattered . . . I think. Straight across the junction here, then bear left.' Anita played a late return of his glance. 'When I introduce you, don't be startled if she comes out with something that sounds . . . what shall I say . . .?'

'Hostile?'

'Cheeky. She has a slight edge to her tongue on occasion, but underneath she's all soft white bread and honey. She's a dear. Far too good,' Anita added fiercely, 'to be conned and rooked by a mob of cheap hustlers who wouldn't help their own grandmothers up off the pavement. It makes my blood boil. I'll move heaven and earth to toss a spanner into their grimy little works.'

'Wow,' said Steve a few minutes later, braking the car at the kerbside. ''You mean she runs this place single-handed?'

'Idiotic, isn't it? She should have sold up years ago. But it's all part of her precious independence, and a game reserve for Ouncey.' Extracting a key from her bag, Anita jumped out and made for the gateway, leaving Steve to follow. Her movements, he noted from the rear, were a mix of coltishness and grace, putting him in mind of his sister before she became a wife and mother and gained in confidence. Removing his gaze with some reluctance, he eyed the scattering of tools and roofing material alongside the porch, and paused to look up. Unable to see, he stepped away from the house to widen the angle. From his new position he had an indistinct view of the roof slates. Much of the expanse was moss-encrusted, apart from a patch at one side, below a ridge, which was a different shade and seemed to be free of fungoid attachments. With a sniff, he joined Anita in the porch.

'They've not exactly flogged themselves to a standstill up there, by the look of it,' he told her as she inserted the key. 'A few square yards might have been replaced, but that's about it. I wonder what they had the gall to charge.'

'Extort, you mean.' Opening the door, she marched through, held it back for him. 'If she's still asleep,' she whispered, closing it softly, 'we can stay in the kitchen for a while and get organized. When she wakes up—'

The sentence broke off. She stood staring along the hall.

'What's up?' he inquired.

'Can you see something on the kitchen floor? I left the door shut. Auntie must have . . .'

She advanced hesitantly. Overtaking her, Steve arrived first, pulled up, recoiled. Putting out an arm, he blocked Anita's progress. Trapped behind him, she made a sound in her throat like a tyre releasing air. 'Oh no,' she wailed. It was the cry of a child, deprived of a promised treat. 'No,' she repeated, as if reiteration would help. 'It *can't* be . . .'

CHAPTER 8

Bella put in an appearance while Dave was having a liquid lunch by himself in the saloon lounge of the Merry Fiddler. She had a lot of acquaintances to greet. When finally she drifted within earshot he pretended not to have noticed her. The scheme backfired. The next time he ventured a glance, she had placed distance between them again, was languidly collecting glasses and ashtrays from remote tables and delivering them to Frankie at the bar. Cursing under his breath, he drifted across.

'Take you out of here in half an hour.'

'No you won't.'

'What?' he said dangerously.

'I'm busy this afternoon. We're short-handed. If you want the pleasure of my company, call back around five, I might be finished by then.'

Frankie smiled at him with faint malice across the bar. Turning his back, Dave fixed Bella briefly with his gimlet look, the one he had practised and perfected over the years. 'You will be,' he said with quiet emphasis.

She looked a shade uncertain. 'What's this, the brush-off?'

'Not if you're smart.' Swigging the last of his beer, Dave slapped the tankard down in front of Frankie with an over-the-shoulder movement and feigned contemplation of the saloon's clientele. As he had hoped, she rose to the bait.

'And assuming I'm smart . . . what then?'

'Have to wait to find out, won't you?'

'I can guess, thanks very much.'

'It's not what you think.'

'Maybe I'm not thinking what you think I'm thinking.'

He shrugged. 'All the same to me. If you want to pass up an opportunity, there's plenty more as won't.'

'Hark at him,' Bella remarked to Frankie. She eyed Dave sidelong. Finally she couldn't restrain herself. 'What sort of an opportunity?'

At the far end of the bar, a tall and trendily-garbed young man with abundant bitter-chocolate hair was observing Bella attentively from the shelter of a whisky glass. Bella, to Dave's certain knowledge, was by no means oblivious of the scrutiny. The previous night, she had ditched her Indian or Pakistani boyfriend without a moment's hesitation, and Dave was in no doubt that she could duplicate the procedure just as readily with anyone else, himself included. She was sure of her powers. He had to box clever. Inclining himself closer, though not too close, he breathed confidentially into her ear.

'Remember that grand I was telling you about?'

'Don't give us a chance to forget, do you? Collected it yet?'

'Never you mind. What I'm saying is, by later on today I might have multiplied that by a few times. In which case, Bella my sweet, I could be feeling lucky. And you know something? I'm the sort of guy who likes to share his luck.'

'Proper philanthropist, in other words.' She eyed him cynically, but she wasn't moving away. Dave kept her on the simmer. Before long she came to the boil. 'This other big job you was talking about?'

'You'll see.'

'Today's Sunday. Don't work on a Sunday, do you?'

'Who said anything about work?'

Bella looked at him doubtfully. 'I don't understand what you're on about. All a bit vague and futuristic, isn't it? I've met your type. Chockfull of promises, but when it comes to delivering the goods . . .'

'Have it your own way,' Dave said indifferently, meeting

the gaze of the chocolate-haired young man and throwing it back in his face. 'Just thought I'd give you the chance, that's all. No sweat. Forget I mentioned it.' He glanced back. 'Fill it up, Frankie, there's a gorgeous fellow. And a Campari for the lady. She might be needing it.'

He stood gazing absently into space. Uncertainty, he was aware without looking at her, had crept into Bella's movements. Itching to express her scepticism, she was nevertheless intrigued enough to put a guard on her tongue, at least for the moment, and to combat the urge to leave him standing. Her orbs flickered in the general direction of the young man at the bar, who remained motionless and watchful. The Campari came at her. Accepting the glass, she took a sip and clasped it to her chest.

'Hate Sunday afternoons, don't you? Nothing ever happens.'

'Depends where you are at the time. And who with.'

'Oh really? What's your method of not getting bored?'

'Stick around and you might find out.'

'If you say so.' Her tone of voice left the matter open. Dave devoted his attention to the beer. Presently Bella added, 'So, what time did you say you was picking us up?'

He smiled, but only to himself. 'Be here at five, Bella my love. Looking your best.'

'Oh, I get it. Only the best is good enough, right?'

He gave her left hip a valedictory pat. 'For some of us.'

Driving too fast along the Barmston road, Dave struggled to thrust images of Bella to the back of his mind while he concentrated on the task in hand.

The quicker he was through, the sooner he'd be back at the Fiddler. From what he had observed as he left, the less delay the better. Something about the stance of the chocolate-haired young man as he ordered another Scotch had indicated to Dave an intention to remain on the scene indefinitely, or for as long as he needed to storm Bella's flimsy defences, and the thought was an unsettling one. Although Dave had done all he knew to stimulate Bella's avarice and curiosity, he cherished no illusions that these factors would necessarily be decisive if and when it came to the crunch. The young whisky-swiller might well come up with a counter-proposition of greater attractiveness, that his quarry might find it impossible to resist.

Over the wheel, Dave muttered resentfully to himself. He had seen the guy paying for his Scotch with a twenty-quid note from his back pocket, where no doubt it had resided with others. Bella, he was convinced, had spotted it too. In present circumstances, it was a hard act to emulate. He, Dave, had a thousand coming to him, and yet for the next few days he was likely to be hard-pressed to lay fingers on a twenty-pence piece, never mind twenty pounds. The tenner he had borrowed in advance from Nigel was virtually spent. In his desperation, Dave had even considered an approach to Vanessa, but had promptly ruled this out. Apart from the fact that it hurt his pride to borrow from his younger sister, it was doubtful whether she could have come across with sufficient to make the exercise worthwhile.

Nigel might have obliged. But Nigel wasn't at home today; or, if he was, he was neglecting to answer the phone.

Would Bella wait? Clearly she was a girl who lived for the moment. Ironically, Dave sympathized. He himself detested waiting. He knew just how Bella felt. The X-factor was, how much in earnest was the young man in the bar: did he contemplate action, or was he one of life's spectators?

Entering Barmston, Dave forced himself to slacken pace through the outlying, leafy residential district. The importance of not drawing attention to himself was paramount. Intent on observing the speed limits, he overshot the junction he was aiming for and lost his bearings for a while, eventually finding his way back to Elm Chase via an adjoining street, Oak Avenue, which took him through to the lower end. In areas like this, he thought with contempt, everybody named their roads after trees. Pathetic. Why didn't they do like Manhattan and tag everything by numbers? Then van drivers would know where they were, no trouble.

Elm Chase, at mid-afternoon on a Sunday, seemed destitute of human life. Taking the van over the footway on to the cindery drive of the house, he parked it alongside the heap of slates and other rubbish they had left lying around for the sake of appearances, and leapt out hastily, in a fever to make headway. Inside the porch, he leaned on the bellpush.

Judging by what he'd seen of her, she was unlikely to be out. The main hazard was that she might have relatives there for tea. Nigel reckoned she was alone in the world, having outlived everyone else: but Nigel could be wrong. Dave rang again. Still no answer.

Swearing under his breath, he walked round to the back of the house, stepping over rusty wire netting on stakes to reach it. At the french window, he shaded out the reflection with a cupped hand while peering through a pane.

The armchair of eccentric design, which he had noticed the old bird make for every time, stood with its back to him. Just beyond it, a slippered foot heel-down on a stool was just visible.

So, she was there. Either she had not heard the doorbell or she was purposely ignoring it. Fury bubbled up inside Dave. Why couldn't people answer the door when summoned?

He rapped imperiously on the glass.

The foot remained motionless. Seizing the door handle, he rattled it mightily, without effect upon either door or foot. By now in a black rage, he pounded the glass with a fist.

'Hoy! You deaf or something?'

Inactivity persisted. He stamped around the uneven flag-stones, raving aloud. Visions of Bella, sloshing back Campari and laughing at the young man's jokes, were driving him demented. How long since he had left her? Half an hour, or more. By the time he got back . . .

On the far side of the tangled lawn, beneath trees, brushwood had accumulated in heaps. Striding across, Dave selected the most solid branch, tore away the attached twigs, returned with it to the door. He jabbed viciously at the middle pane.

The noise was like an explosion. The glass shattered inwards. Completing the clearance with his right elbow, Dave inserted a hand and fumbled at the door catch, without result. Below it, a key protruded from the woodwork. He turned it back, a revolution and a half.

While he was doing this, he noticed that the foot had vanished. At a higher level, a face was now peering at him around the wing of the armchair. To Dave's satisfaction, it expressed stark terror. Giving the door handle a wrench, he put weight against it, felt the door yield a little. He thrust harder. Freed of its swollen frame, the door burst inwards, enabling him to make an entrance as intimidating as it was dramatic. The flurry of violent action was a solace. A few more seconds of frustration, Dave felt, and he would literally have exploded in all directions.

The old creature was encased in a thick, fleecy dressing-gown, but underneath, he could see, she was fully clad. Her mouth opened and closed, like a herring's. Plainly she was half-paralysed by fear and shock. Striking while the iron was hot, Dave addressed her from close range, his voice pitched on a Wagnerian scale.

'Remember me, Mrs Holwood? The roofing engineer? Got bad news for you, I'm afraid. It's about your dog.'

With shaking hands, she was trying to bring herself more

upright in the chair. Every vestige of colour had drained
from her cheeks, giving her the appearance of an effigy in
crumpled white plastic, with button eyes. Wheezing sounds
came from her chest. Looming over her, Dave planted both
hands on the chair-arms.

'Not too good, he isn't. Needs a few more of them pills, I
reckon. Got any handy?'

Maisie's head shook. She seemed to be trying to clear
it, rather than answer him. 'Fast asleep, was you?' Dave
inquired. 'Sunday afternoon kip? All right for the leisured
classes. Sorry I had to bust a way in, like, only it was urgent,
see? The dog's not looking too clever.'

Maisie let out a moan. 'Has he got something to drink?'

'Drink?' Dave simulated surprise. 'Never thought of that.
What does he have? Tea, water . . .?'

'He must take fluid. He'll die without it.'

'I'll try to remember that.'

'Where is he?' Maisie had struggled into a stiff-backed
position, but was still fighting for breath. 'Where are you
keeping him?'

'Safe place, Mrs Holwood, no problem. Tell you what,
though. Pricey business, keeping him fed an' that. Cost us
a packet already, I can tell you.'

'Can't you bring him back here? Then I could—'

'I *would*,' Dave said reasonably. 'Only I'm still a bit
bothered re the security aspect. If you know what I mean.'

Her head shook again in despair. 'I *don't* know what you
mean. Security? What is it you're talking about?'

Dave clicked his tongue. 'Thought Nigel had made it all
clear to you, Mrs Holwood. Collateral for the work and
materials. You understood that, didn't you?'

From her eyes, he inferred that she was striving without
much success to make sense of his words. 'Now then,' he
went on, talking deliberately despite the temptation to rush
it, 'if you was to authorize another little payment on account,

we'd be laughing, right? This time tomorrow, you'd have your dog back here where he belongs, noshing his water and his tablets. See what I'm getting at? It's all down to you.'

'You've had six thousand already. Isn't that enough?'

'Three, we've had.'

'Six,' she insisted.

'You're just trying to . . .' Dave paused. 'Six, was it?' he resumed on a softer key. 'Okay, darling. I believe you. But we've not got it yet. That cheque of yours could bounce next week, for all we know.'

'It's from the building society.'

'Still . . . not the same as cash, is it? Not nearly the same. Come across with a few of the readies and I'd be a whole lot happier. The dog, too. Pining for his mistress he is, I reckon, something terrible. Breaks your heart to listen to him.'

'You *must* bring him back to me.'

'On an exchange basis.'

A wail broke from Maisie. 'If I give you another cheque—'

'Sorry, darling. It's cash or nothing.'

'Fetch me my purse.'

She pointed to her bag on the table. Reaching for it, Dave said idly, 'Carry much about, do you? Watch out for muggers, I would.'

'I don't keep a lot . . .' Tugging at the clasp, Maisie found her purse and somehow got it open, peered frantically into the compartments. 'Pound coins—will they do? How many do you want? Take it all.' She pressed the purse on him.

Dave steered it aside. 'Not a lot of use to me, darling, I'm afraid. Where's the real lolly?'

'The real . . .? I don't . . . I'm not . . .'

'Come on,' said Dave, controlling his temper. 'Keep it in the house, don't you? For bills an' that. Just tell us where I'll find it and we're in business.'

'I haven't any. There's none here.'

'Last chance,' he said steadily, leaning forward to bring his face within inches of hers. 'Tell us where to look. Upstairs, is it?'

'You must believe me,' she stammered. 'I'm not trying to deceive you, Dave. That's right, isn't it? I've got your name right? I never keep money in the house. They told me not to.'

'Who did? The bank? Don't trust banks, do you? People like you don't have anything to do with banks.'

Maisie's uncomprehending stare tilted him over the edge. He gripped her by the shoulders, making her gasp, then cry out. '*Do* you, you old faggot? Want your dog back? In one piece? All right, then. Show us where you keep the bloody stuff. You're wasting my time.'

Choking sounds came out of her. Slackening his fingers, Dave administered a sharp slap to the jawbone, sending her head to one side. 'No sense holding out on us. You'll come clean in the end. Look, darling, we both know you've got cash in the house—stands to reason. So why not save me and yourself a load of hassle? All you have to do is tell us where it is. I'll find it, anyway, in the end,' he added, in the tone of a logician addressing a seminar.

Her face, he noticed with casual interest, was changing rapidly in colour from ash to yellow to deep red, and finally to a kind of purple. The clock on the mantelpiece caught his eye. Three-forty, it said. So far, this mission had taken him well over the hour. By the time he made it back to the Fiddler, would Bella be gone? In a renewal of fever he dealt Maisie another slap, adding to the suffusion of her facial flesh.

'Come on!' he shouted. Reclaiming her shoulders, he shook her like a dust-saturated rug. 'Can't stick around here, can I, while you make up your stupid mind? Where d'you keep it?'

There was no response and no resistance: it was like handling a bagful of bones. In an abrupt fury of exasperation, Dave wrenched her one-handed out of the chair, slammed her against the table-edge. Physical pain, in Dave's experience, was something readily grasped by most people. It got results. More quickly, more effectively than all this psychological stuff that characters like Nigel were fond of spouting about. Dave's own aversion to bodily discomfort was a yardstick: it enabled him to appreciate the effect it was likely to have upon others.

In this instance, the results seemed to be delayed. After hitting the table, Maisie had slumped gracelessly to the carpet to lie in an uncommunicative mound. Beside himself with wrath and impatience, Dave picked her up and carried her out to the kitchen. The place was neat and clean. For some reason, this infuriated him further. It wouldn't have surprised him to learn that she had a home help in most days, paid for out of that hoard which she was refusing to tell him about. A dousing might bring her to her senses. Hoisting her across the sink, he held her face-upward beneath the left-hand tap and ran it full force into her nose and eyes, waiting to hear her splutter.

The effect was a let-down. Maisie remained inert in his arms, her eyes open but unfocused, her lips apart and yet saying nothing. Playing dumb, was she?

He knew a way to find out. Carrying her back to the centre of the kitchen, he lifted her head-high and let go.

She landed with a thud that should have jerked some kind of a squeak out of her. Still she refused to cooperate. 'For Christ's sake!' For the moment, he was regardless of possible neighbours. 'Why can't you say something, you stupid old cow?'

Leaving her there, he ran upstairs to the first landing, stood looking feverishly around. Which room first? In a place this size, she might keep her savings anywhere: finding it could take him hours, and he hadn't that sort of time to spare. Bella was slipping out of reach. Near to despair, he flung open the nearest door, to be confronted by a room infested by cupboard doors and old furniture: just to get through this one would have taken him the rest of the afternoon. Useless. He stormed back downstairs.

The posture of Maisie on the kitchen floor had not altered. Dropping to his knees, Dave brought his mouth close to her ear. 'Wake up!' he bawled, digging her in the ribs with a vigour that, again, should have produced results but didn't. The old hulk remained obdurate. And now, as well as time, he had run out of ideas. There was nothing more he could do. If he wanted to reclaim Bella, he had to get back.

'And I hope you're bloody satisfied,' he snarled, before leaving.

On the way back, he spotted a bungalow in its own grounds with one of its front windows half-open. Taking the van boldly into the drive, he leapt out and pounded the brass door-knocker: no reply. Silence from within. No dogs. Sauntering to the window, he pulled it wide open and swarmed through into a kind of study with a desk across one corner. Without much hope, he dragged out a couple of drawers. At the back of the second he found a brown plastic wallet encircled by a rubber band: inside was a bunch of fifty-pound notes. In a daze, he pocketed the money before returning swiftly to the van. Nobody was around. Evergreens blocked the view from surrounding properties. Like lifting sweets from a supermarket, he thought, driving away.

CHAPTER 9

'We'll nail the bastard,' vowed Detective-Sergeant Bennett.

The remark was addressed to Steve across the bowed head of Anita, who was clutching but not drinking half a glassful of brandy. 'Whoever it was,' he added, eyeing her compassionately, 'he's no pro, that's for sure. Left his trademarks all over the shop.'

'Did he take much?'

'Can't say. Unless Miss Blythe here can tell us any more about her aunt's circumstances . . . We don't know if she kept valuables in the house.'

Anita looked up. 'She hadn't any. She lived on her pensions.'

The sergeant frowned. 'As I understand it, though, she implied to you that she'd paid these men off for her dog?'

'Yes. But I've no idea how much.'

'If and when we find her cheque book . . . You don't happen to know where she banked?'

'Until she mentioned a cheque, I never knew she had an account.'

'Feel up to getting home now, Miss Blythe?'

'Isn't there something more I can do? You must be—'

'Anything else can wait till tomorrow.' He helped her gently out of the chair, one of the few items of furniture remaining in Maisie's long-abandoned front room, formerly used at mealtimes and on social occasions. 'The Chief Inspector and maybe the Chief Super will want to see you then, but in the meantime I suggest you take it easy and get over the shock.' He gave Steve a glance. 'Staying with her?'

'You bet.'

'I feel so helpless.' Anita looked vacantly at the door leading to the hall. 'Helpless and guilty.'

'Guilty?' echoed the sergeant. 'How come?'

'I could have prevented it.'

'How, for God's sake?' demanded Steve.

'By being here.'

'You were only gone a couple of hours. You couldn't possibly have foreseen . . . It was sheer dreadful luck.'

'Mr Walsh is right, Miss Blythe. No use blaming yourself.'

Anita looked from one to the other. 'Isn't that what people always say?'

After an uncomfortable silence Bennett went to the door. 'I'll be getting back to the station. The scene-of-crime lads will be here for a while yet, and we don't want to cramp their style. We'll see you first thing in the morning. Both of you.' He paused to look back. 'Should anything spectacular come up before then, I'll give you a buzz.'

'Will you?'

'Of course. And *don't* stop on here, Miss Blythe, reproaching yourself. You did all the right things. Events moved too fast for us, that's all there is to it.'

'If I'd just called in on her a week earlier . . .'

'You'd have been equally powerless to prevent it,' Sergeant Bennett said forthrightly. 'All the while your aunt was alone in this house—and she was here by choice, don't forget: nobody made her stay here—she was an elderly female person at risk, and there's no getting away from it. Which doesn't make things any easier for you, I realize. Try to get some sleep tonight. Got any tablets?'

'Probably. Somewhere.'

'Down a couple. Put yourself under. Help get you through till daylight.'

'You'll never get any sleep on that. I'll be fine, really. Call for me in the morning.'

'That sofa,' observed Steve, eyeing it expertly, 'would outshine the average seat in an air terminal . . . and I've slept on plenty of those. I'm perfectly happy to stay.' He stood looking at her. 'If you *want* company, that is.'

'I'm not sure.' She gave him a wan smile. 'Yes, I am. I'd like you to stay.'

'Okay. Matter settled.'

'But I'll take the sofa. You sleep in my bed.'

'What do you take me for?'

'A sensible bloke,' she said quickly. 'I shan't sleep, whatever happens. Pills won't help. So I might just as well sit up all night and . . . do a crossword or something, while you get some proper rest. No, please don't argue. I'd prefer it that way. Like some coffee?'

'I'll make some.'

'Let me. It's something to keep me occupied.'

Conceding the point, Steve sat in the spare armchair and listened to the sounds she made in the kitchen, trying not to recall the sight that had met them in Maisie's. He was still in partial shock. What was Anita's present condition? He could only guess. She was now a little too calm, too self-possessed for his liking. Hysterics he would have found easier to cope with. When she reappeared with two beakers and a sugar bowl, he had still formulated no plan for dealing with her; but fortunately she saved him the trouble. Seating herself opposite him, she passed him one of the beakers and the sugar, then stayed leaning forward, regarding him thoughtfully. Presently she said, 'There's no instant antidote, is there, to something like this?'

He shook his head. 'Nope.'

'A year from now, I shall still be seeing her lying there . . .'

'Try not to dwell on it.'

She nursed her beaker. 'Know what I'd like?'

'What?' he said uneasily.

Anita stared into vacancy. 'I'd like them to catch this

man . . . or these men. Then I'd like to be put in a room
with them. A special room. They'd be one side of an invisible
screen: I'd be the other. They could see me, but not get at
me. But I could get at them.'

She looked back, eyes gleaming. 'Do things to them. Very
gradually, bit by bit. Electronic things. Then, when they
were thoroughly dismantled . . .'

She paused to reflect. Steve said in embarrassment, 'It's
natural you should feel this way. Most people would, I
imagine.'

'Only you don't approve?'

'Who am I to pass judgement? You're entitled to feel
bitter.'

'But thoughts of vengeance? Not healthy?'

Steve lifted his shoulders. 'They probably have some
therapeutic effect, in the aftermath.'

'At some stage, though, you're meant to shrug them
off?'

'If it were me . . .'

'Yes? If it were you?'

'I think I incline to the fatalistic. What's done is done.'

'Take no action, you mean, to prevent a recurrence? Is
that what you're saying?'

'I hope not. I'd expect the police to do all in their power
to track the culprit down. As I'm sure they will. My point
is—'

'Having nabbed him, don't make him suffer?'

'Not if you're an interested party. It has to be dispassion-
ate.'

Anita shook her head. 'Sorry. I don't see it. To my mind,
that's just what it shouldn't be. Let's not argue about it.
First he has to be tracked down, this subhuman, and despite
what the police said it may be trickier than they think,
because what do they have to go on? Unless he was seen by
someone . . .'

'Even if he was, a description might not be that helpful if he doesn't have a record. I agree, in a case of this sort the cops are up against it. This is where you come in, Anita.' Steve groped in a pocket, produced a small pad and a ballpen. 'Best thing you can do right now, I'd say, is to ransack your memory.' He passed her the pen and paper. 'Every last detail your Great-Aunt Maisie let slip to you about those roofing cowboys—put it down. Then hand it all to the CID. It could help.'

'I've told them everything I know.'

'I doubt it. You couldn't have been thinking straight when they questioned you. Once you start scribbling, other things will come back.'

'You think so?'

'Try it, anyhow. I'll be making sandwiches. Okay by you?'

'Help yourself. Not for me, though. I couldn't touch a crumb.'

When he returned from the kitchen she was writing furiously, covering the fourth sheet. Closing the door quietly, Steve planted the sandwich plate alongside her left elbow, took one for himself and ate it while scanning the *Sunday Bugle* on the sofa. Presently he saw her take a bite out of one of the sandwiches as she scrawled.

He felt relief. Her rigid exterior self-control had begun to bother him: it seemed unnatural, and surely unhealthy. Steve was a great believer in the healing power of the written word, and it was for this reason, rather than any hope of a dramatic breakthrough, that he had suggested she put her recollections down on paper. Privately, he doubted whether anything that Auntie Maisie had confided would prove to be of much help to the police; but he wasn't going to say so. As if tuned in to his thoughts, Anita glanced across.

'A lot of this is trivia, I guess. Will the police mind having it shoved at them?'

'Why should they? They ought to be grateful. Don't forget, Anita—what seems irrelevant to you might be just the lead they're looking for. Amazing how one thing leads to another. Don't give up.'

'Who's giving up? I'm seeing this through to the bitter end. I owe it to Auntie Maisie.'

He watched her in silence as she completed her dossier, read it through, made a few alterations, finally replaced the cap of the ballpen and handed it back to him. Clipping the sheets together, she folded them into her bag. 'I'll take it along now.'

'Morning will do,' he protested.

'A few hours could make a vital difference.'

'Maybe you're right. I'll be turning the car . . .'

'No, Steve. I think I'd sooner walk there by myself. Do you mind?'

'Of course not. I understand. But watch your step.'

'I'll see it gets to one of the investigating officers.' Accepting the dossier, the station sergeant spread it on the reception counter and glanced down the topmost sheet. 'Very thoughtful of you, Miss . . . Blythe. Might well be a gem of information tucked away in there.'

'That's what I'm hoping.' Anita coughed. 'I'd like the Chief Superintendent to have it.'

'He'll see it all right, I've no doubt.'

'I want it handed to him personally, as soon as possible. Will you do that?'

'Leave it with me,' the sergeant said tolerantly.

'I don't want it left with you. I want him to have it, now.'

He gave her a second look. 'There'll be no unnecessary delay, madam, I promise you.' He glanced back at the dossier. 'Your aunt, was it?'

'Great-aunt.'

'Fairly close, were you?'

'Miles apart,' said Anita. 'Just when she needed me.'

The sergeant wagged an avuncular head. 'No use scolding yourself over a thing like that. If each one of us—'

'I'm not scolding myself. Not any more. I'm trying to compensate.'

'That's the spirit.'

'So you'll get that to the top man for me?'

'The top man. Right this minute.'

'Is he a good detective?'

'Chief Super? One of the best. He came to us from—'

'I want the very best there is.'

'All I can tell you is, he's one of these people who take the utmost—'

'Could I see him?'

The sergeant surveyed her kindly. 'Not just now you can't, I'm afraid. If he needs to—'

'Why not?'

'Mm?'

'Why can't I see him? I was her only relative. He ought to be talking to me.'

'When the time comes, I'm sure he'll be doing just that.'

'The time is now, I'd have thought. Before the scent grows cold.'

'In a murder investigation,' explained the sergeant, looking about him a little huntedly, 'you'll find there's generally a standard routine adopted by the investigating team. It seldom pays to deviate. To the lay person it may seem cumbersome, but it does frequently get results. Now, if the Chief Super were to take time out to interview you tonight, it could mean him neglecting some other line of inquiry . . . maybe a more promising one. See what I'm driving at? He has to—'

'What you're really saying, he's gone home to supper and left word that he's not to be disturbed?'

The sergeant loitered a moment over his reply. 'A man

heading an inquiry,' he said at last, deliberately, 'needs to pace himself. Otherwise he'll crack up. That wouldn't help anybody, would it?'

'Least of all my great-aunt.'

'Exactly.'

'She's beyond help, anyway. It's too late.'

'Sadly, one has to recognize—'

'But we might prevent some other catastrophe if we can get this thug in the next day or so. Don't you think?'

'In this business,' said the sergeant, his lips judicially pursed, 'you have to be realistic. See, it's not like your average domestic squabble, ending in violence. There, you know who's involved. In cases like this, needles in haystacks, the most you can do—'

'That sounds very defeatist.'

'Let me put it another way . . . Got a minute, sir?' the sergeant interrupted himself, straightening with manifest relief to signal to a youngish man in plain clothes who was passing through in a hurry. 'I've Miss Blythe with me. She was anxious—'

'Miss Who?'

'Blythe. She'd like to see the Chief Super, but he's non-available just now, as you know. Maybe you'd like a word with her yourself?

Pivoting on a heel, the plainclothes man came across, brow puckered. 'Is it to do with the Wilkins case?'

'Not that one, sir. The assault on Mrs Holwood. Miss Blythe here is her nearest relative.'

'Ah. The niece who found her. Chief Inspector Brian Davison,' the CID man introduced himself, placing an elbow on the counter-flap and pursuing it with his weight. 'Got some fresh information for us, Miss Blythe?'

'Great-niece, actually. She was elderly, you know, and frail.'

'Quite,' he said solemnly.

'I've written a lot of stuff down. I thought it might help the Chief Superintendent if he read it.'

'Fine. Good thinking.'

'But he probably won't see it until tomorrow, I gather?'

'Depends. He's currently up to his eyes, you can imagine. Where is it?'

Silently the sergeant passed him the dossier. Davison ran an eye down the first page. 'Nicely thorough, Miss Blythe,' he observed, tucking the bundle away in a pocket. 'I'll make sure that it gets an airing.'

Anita gazed at him. 'Tonight?'

'I don't know about that. We've several things on.'

'More important than the savaging of an old lady?'

'It's not so much a question of *importance*,' Davison explained patiently. 'More a matter of priorities. What we have to—'

'By tomorrow, anything of value in that document could be totally out of date.'

'I think you'll find we're doing all we can. We've got the forensic squad working inside and outside the house, we've got the inquiry team talking to the neighbouring—'

'Nobody's talking to me.'

'Don't I count as somebody?' he asked whimsically. 'I'm ready to listen. Let's have it, Miss Blythe.'

She looked dumbly down at her hands. The two men waited, exchanging glances. Suddenly, with a headshake, Anita grabbed her bag and hurried out. The sergeant released a heavy sigh.

'Takes 'em that way, sometimes.'

'Can't altogether blame them, Charlie, I suppose.' Davison paused to rub fatigue out of his eyes. 'To their way of thinking, it's logical to assume that the entire strength of the local force should be allocated to their particular case for as long as it takes. How d'you explain to them we've got fifteen others, equally atrocious, jostling for attention?'

'To say nothing of a manpower shortage,' the sergeant said bleakly. 'My advice to you, sir, is don't even try. Save your energy for the villains.'

'Were they glad to have it?'

'I've no idea,' said Anita. 'They didn't say.'

She went through to the bathroom. Steve heard the tap running, and splashing sounds: then there was a prolonged silence. A little uneasy, he tapped on the door.

'All right in there?'

'I'll be out in a sec.'

She emerged a minute later, having done, he observed, quite a lot to her face, which had been white and tense when she came in. Colour and lipstick had been applied, and she had also done something to her hair. Steve lifted the coffee pot questioningly. Shaking her head, she sat at the table and set to work on her nails, filing and varnishing. There was a certain abnormal intensity to her manner. Half refilling his beaker, Steve sat stirring in sugar.

'You mean to tell me they didn't even acknowledge the damn thing?'

'Oh, they thanked me nicely. In a couple of days' time, someone there will have read a good half of it, I shouldn't wonder.'

'They're not taking you seriously?'

'Only the distressed great-niece, aren't I? Just one of the people who found her body. Why talk to me?'

'To be fair,' Steve said objectively, 'you've been interviewed. You were asked—'

'I've spoken to a sergeant: and then briefly to an inspector. Now, I've had a few futile words with a *chief* inspector. I'm working my way up. By this time next week I should have reached the top man, by which time . . .'

Recapping the varnish bottle, she returned it to her bag, swivelled in her chair to face him. 'I expect I'm being unreasonably demanding. Merely mortal, aren't they, the police? It's like so many things. You expect the plumber or the electrician to dash along with instant service and trace the fault at once . . . but how often does it happen? No wonder there's an upsurge in DIY.'

'By and large,' Steve suggested, 'I guess the professionals do their best.'

'That's what bothers me.' Grasping the remote control, Anita switched on the TV. 'Shall we see what's on?'

Steve showed his alarm. 'It's the regional news, I think, after the main bulletin. You don't want to—'

'Yes I do. I'd like to hear what they have to say.'

Two presenters, male and female, were sitting at desks and talking jokily between themselves about the weather. After a minute of this, the male of the pair turned back to Camera One and became grave. 'Police,' he intoned, 'are hunting for an intruder who earlier today carried out a violent attack upon an elderly widow at her home in Chapleigh, four miles from Barmston. Frail Mrs Maisie Holwood, who weighed only six stone, died from her injuries. Motive for the break-in is believed to have been robbery, but it's not yet known whether anything was taken. Mrs Holwood's Yorkshire terrier . . .'

'Switch it off,' urged Steve.

Anita watched the item to its conclusion before flicking the life out of the set. She sat motionless, her gaze remaining upon the blank screen. Irresolutely, Steve rose and took the beakers and sandwich plate back to the kitchen, rinsed them clean, stacked them, inspected the refrigerator contents; then, suddenly decisive, returned to the living-room.

'Look, I'm serving no useful purpose here and you might prefer to be by yourself for a bit. If I went back to my flat, you could call me if—'

'You are serving a purpose, Steve. I'm glad to have you around.' Her dark eyes fixed themselves upon him. 'Maybe you'd rather go back, though? I'm causing you a lot of inconvenience?'

'Good God, no. I'm happy to stay, if it's helpful. I just don't want you to feel I'm getting under your heels, that's all.'

'If I felt that, I'd have said so by now. I'd prefer you to stay,' she added prosaically, 'as long as it's not interfering too much with your own routine. Do say, if it is. I shan't mind. I'll quite understand.'

'What makes you think I study a routine?' He gave her a tentative grin. 'Wild Man Walsh—that's what I'm known as in sedate circles. One of the great uncommitted. If you want me, I'm yours for the night.'

She didn't blink. 'All right, it's a deal. What time do you want to be called in the morning?'

'Any time that suits. My next overseas trip isn't until Wednesday.' He hesitated. 'Have you changed your mind about turning in?'

'No. You're welcome to the bed. I'll stay in here and play Scrabble with myself.'

He came back to the table. 'Get the board out. Tenpence for fifty points?'

She stared. 'You don't have to, you know.'

'What do you mean, I don't have to? I'm a sucker for the game. You're up against the Editorial All-Comers Champion, as it happens, so you'd better bring out the dictionary.' He sat facing her. 'Don't know about you, but I find it takes the mind off things.'

CHAPTER 10

'Motive for the break-in,' said the newscaster, 'is believed to have been robbery, but it's not yet known whether anything was taken. Mrs Holwood's Yorkshire terrier is understood to be missing from the house, and it's thought likely that he was scared off by the violence. The man leading the hunt, Detective Chief Superintendent Roger Malling, said that Mrs Holwood was of a somewhat reclusive nature, with few living relatives, and it had been difficult to establish whether or not she was in the habit of keeping cash or valuables in the house. One theory—'

'Hear what I said?' Dave jogged Bella's elbow.

'I was just listening to that.' She nodded at the TV screen glinting at them from the bar of the Club Marseille, which notwithstanding its surface glitz was starting to grate on her nerves. The Sunday evening clientele was hardly what Dave had led her to expect. Where were the youngsters, the swingers? Nobody around them seemed to be under sixty. And all of them were behaving with tedious decorum over bottles of blameless wine. Such dancing as was in progress had been devised for narcolepts. Keyed for action, Bella had found herself slumping by degrees into a condition bordering upon stupor, not alleviated by the boastful reminiscences of her escort as he plied her with something described on the label as Dom Perignon, although Bella wasn't fooled. She recognized a switch when she tasted one. This place was nothing but a costly dive for gullible senior citizens. Could Dave possibly imagine she was impressed?

'Enjoy punishing yourself, do you?' he queried sulkily.

'You're meant to keep up with events.' Releasing herself from his enfolding arm, she placed several inches between her body and his. 'I do try to take an interest. Though personally, I could do without some of the things you hear about.' In the absence of fun, she reflected, they might as well have a sober discussion on things that counted. 'Too much casual violence around these days, if you ask me.'

'Nobody's asking you.'

'Well, maybe they should. What about that poor defenceless ninety-year-old they've just been telling us of? Living by herself, doing nobody any harm . . . then along comes some twisted psychopath whose only thought—'

'D'you have to go on about it? We're here to enjoy ourselves.'

'You could have fooled me.'

'What's that supposed to mean?'

'It's supposed to mean I'd never have believed it. For once in a while, I'm more hooked by that screen than I am by real life. If—' Bella gazed about her in wonderment—'you can call this life. By my reckoning, this lot died quietly in their sleep after they'd all had their Sunday dinners. What we've got here is a load of walking corpses, waiting for the undertaker.'

'You wanted to go somewhere. This is somewhere.'

'I'd noticed that. Reminds me of a motorway service area. A place along the route. I've had more laughs in a supermarket.'

She turned to eye him. 'That how you treat all your lady friends? Knock 'em about a bit?'

'I've spent cash on you tonight.'

'Oh, so that's what rankles. How'd you come by it, anyhow? One minute you're skint: the next—'

'I told you. A business deal.'

'Get away. You're hardly the type, Dave Forester, to sign agreements in the middle of a Sunday afternoon.' She became thoughtful. 'Debt-collection . . .'

'Huh?'

'Hustling the non-payers. You'd be good at that, I should imagine. Paying game, too. Something on those lines, Dave? Some nice little gainful racket?'

'You could be getting warm,' he told her enigmatically. 'When there's something to collect, I collect.'

'I bet. Like whoever did that poor old woman in. She probably had something—'

'Will you forget about that?' he shouted.

Heads turned at nearby tables. One or two revellers, to Bella's chagrin, swapped smiles: the rest looked stuffy, which was worse. She had almost had enough.

'Don't you take that tone with me,' she hissed fiercely. 'What are you so touchy about? Just another victim, isn't she? Nothing special about her.' Her eyes narrowed. 'Or is there?'

'Now what is it?''

'I'm not sure.' Maintaining space between them, she was examining his facial skin as though analysing it for dermatitis: which was odd, in a way, because Dave really was starting to feel as if symptoms of some cutaneous complaint were displaying themselves on his features. 'Not known you long, have I? The Man of Mystery. Never says what he's up to. Gets hysterical at newscasts. Funny, that. I took you for the laid-back sort.'

Dave settled back in a relaxed manner. 'Like you said, it's the violence. Too much of it around. People like that . . .' He nodded at the screen. '. . . they want putting inside for keeps.'

Bella made scoffing noises. 'Shoving through a mincer, more like. Might bring it home to them.'

'Wouldn't solve anything.'

'Clear 'em out the way, wouldn't it? Make space for a few half-decent types to step in and take over. Everyone's sick to death hearing about these savages and what they get up to.'

'Stop rabbiting on about it, then.'

'Why should I? Just to please you? There *is* something,' Bella added, observing him still more closely. 'What is it, Dave? You know something about who might've been responsible?'

''Course I don't.'

'You're in with a few funny guys. I've seen you talking. Who's the bloke with the natty suits and the fancy cravats?'

'Nigel? He's not that type.'

'No, but I wouldn't put it past him to have the basic idea and leave others to do his dirty work. What's he do for a living?'

'Search me. Are we here to enjoy ourselves?' Dave demanded, pouring champagne recklessly into their glasses, 'or have a debate on city crime?'

'Depends what you call enjoying yourself.' Still Bella had not taken her eyes off him. 'What's your idea of enjoyment, Dave? Beating up old ladies?'

'You trying to be funny?'

'I can be a lot funnier than that, without trying. It just struck me, that's all. You'd have had time.'

'Time for what?'

'You were gone a couple of hours this afternoon. Then you came back with fifty-quid notes spilling out of your socks. A business deal, you said. Okay. What kind of a deal?'

'I don't think I want to discuss that with you, Bella.'

'You were keen enough to talk about it last night. What's the sudden objection?'

Dave resettled himself into an attitude of moderation. 'Yeah, well, you've got me cornered. It was me. She reminded me of my mum, so I thumped her a few times, then took the meter money. Dead easy.'

'I suppose you think *that's* funny.' Sipping slowly from her glass, Bella continued to contemplate him over its rim. 'You know, Dave,' she resumed presently, evading in a feline way the physical contact he was trying to establish with an arm, 'I've read of other cases, every bit as nasty. Solitary old folk with hoards of cash in biscuits tins on the—'

'Maybe you read too much.'

Bella stared down at the shiny evening bag in her lap, glanced at him again. 'So, where did the fifties come from?

The other party you were doing this deal with?'

'That's it, love. The other party. If it's any of your business.'

'Seeing as I'm helping to spend it, perhaps it is partly my business. I wouldn't want to . . .' Bella paused. 'Don't know a lot about you, Dave, do I?'

'Come to that, I'm no authority on you.'

'You've only got to ask. *I've* nothing to hide. Not shown much interest though, have you, up to now? Not that sort of interest.'

'First things first, my motto.' The grin essayed by Dave wobbled badly off course, skidded into oblivion. There was a moment's silence.

'I'm twenty-six and single,' said Bella on recital mode. 'My mum lives in New Zealand. I help out my old man at the pub. I get paid out of the profits and I like a good time. That's about it. You've got it all, there.'

'Thanks a heap.'

'Now it's your turn.'

'You're not interested in my history.'

'You're right, I'm not. When I go out with a bloke, though, I don't like it when he curls up tighter than woodlice every time I ask a question. Makes me twitchy.'

'Don't ask questions, then.'

Bella took a breath. 'Just one more. How soon can we get out of this dump?'

Dave's knuckles whitened. 'What's wrong with it?'

'Nothing that a couple of well-placed bombs couldn't put to rights. Take us home, will you? I've spent livelier evenings doing the ironing.'

Rising silently, Dave walked off towards the exit.

Emulating him at a statelier pace after struggling into her white, simulated fur jacket and putting her hairstyle through a perfunctory remould, Bella ignored haughtily the inquisitive glances of those at surrounding tables and click-clacked her way half a mile, it seemed, to the door, hiccuping under her breath from the effects of the alcohol. Outside, in the asphalt wilderness of a car park, Dave was sitting at the wheel of the van, dragging on a cigarette. Opening the passenger door, she installed herself and sat back, arms folded across the seat harness.

Dave flicked ash through his open window. Having reduced the cigarette to half its length, he did likewise with the remnant before sparking the engine and driving off jerkily into the street, narrowly avoiding a brace of cars that chanced to be passing. Regaining a straight course, he chuntered to the first junction and turned right. Bella eyed the signposts.

'You're going the wrong way.'

'Just as quick.' His tone, to her surprise, was quite amiable. She relaxed slightly. In twenty minutes she would be back home, and that was going to be the end of Dave Forester as far as she was concerned. Ready cash or no ready cash, his company was not exactly a turn-on: besides which, she prided herself on not being a good-time girl at any price. She had her standards. Dad would laugh about her dreary evening, when she told him.

'Where d'you hang out?' she asked, to make conversation.

'More questions?' Still there was no resumption of the hostility. 'Got an apartment in Petgrove. Ten minutes from the shops.'

'An apartment? You mean a room?'

'Do I?'

'An apartment is a flat. How many rooms you got?'

'Enough to be going on with.' Reducing speed, he tucked in behind a heavy goods vehicle that was hugging the nearside verge of the dual-track highway that led out of the city towards Barmston. 'Doesn't come cheap, I'll tell you. Had a rent rise last week.'

'Shouldn't bother you. All this loot coming in.'

'Still think I'm the far side of the law, eh Bella?'

'None of my business. You said so yourself.'

With a shrug, he concentrated on the tail lights of the vehicle ahead. Bella sighed to herself. For a short while she'd had hopes of him, but once again she seemed to have slipped up. She was starting to mistrust her judgement. The only course, she knew from hard-won experience, was to cut her losses and begin yet again. Ever the optimist, Bella knew she would achieve her ideal eventually: it was just a matter of persistence. Never give up.

For the moment, her one aim was to remove herself from Dave's proximity. There was something not quite wholesome about him.

Apart from which, she wasn't mad about his driving. 'Staying a bit close, aren't you?' she ventured, as the tail lights they were following came back at them in a somewhat alarming lunge. 'Better watch out for the breathalysers.'

Dave said nothing. He did, however, drop back a few yards, veering in the process and half-mounting the grass verge before regaining the tarmac and motoring on, seemingly unaware of his lapse. Apprehension seized Bella. He must be tighter than he had appeared. How many glassfuls of the lousy champagne had he consumed? Doing her best to recall, she failed to notice, or at least to register, that his left hand had deserted the wheel to fumble with something between the seats, something that responded with a faint clunk before the hand returned to its former position, doing its bit towards the van's increasingly erratic progress. It was now proceeding in a series of open-ended loops. Passing traffic was flashing its headlamps. Bella gripped the ledge in front of her.

'Ease up, Dave. Hear what I said? You'll have us in the ditch.'

His unnerving silence stayed intact. Was he in a drunken

trance? Leaning across to grab the wheel, she was conscious
of a greater freedom of movement than she had expected,
but in the confusion of the moment there was no time to
investigate. Her entire attention was focused on survival.
'Brake!' she shrieked into his ear. 'Put the brakes on, you
lunatic! D'you want to—'

His left hand moved again, faster this time, knocking her
away.

Lurching against the nearside door, she realized dizzily
what it was that she had sensed about her position on the
seat. It was untrammelled by the seat-belt. Somehow, the
locking mechanism had come adrift. Fighting to get herself
upright, she was again flung to the side as the van swerved
and bounced, its nearside wheels gouging the turf.

Ahead, the goods vehicle was pulling away. To the left,
the outline of a hedgerow loomed out of the dusk. Between
them and the foliage, Bella knew, was a dyke. She had taken
this road before. An embankment ran down to the water.
The van seemed to be heading straight for it. Clawing
at handholds, she opened her mouth to bawl at Dave
again.

'Give it a good blow, sir, will you?'

Like a good citizen, Dave complied. When he had finished, the traffic cop removed the breathalyser equipment
and told him to stay where he was. He did so, observing the
activity, keeping both arms under the blanket they had
draped round him as he half sat on, half leaned against the
grit container at the roadside.

The non-stop, blue flashing light of the police car lit up
the scene on the verge, where two or three uniformed figures
were crouched over a motionless form hidden by what looked
like a small tarpaulin. Presently a distant howling sound
reached Dave's ears. Another blue light, pulsing rather than
flashing. Turning off skilfully to bounce the ambulance

into place alongside the police Rover, the driver leapt out, pursued by his mate, and joined the team assembled on the wet grass. Other traffic, meanwhile, continued to thunder incuriously past.

The officer returned to Dave. 'Best get inside the ambulance, sir. Have a check-up at the hospital.'

'Right you are, ta.'

''Fraid I've bad news about your passenger.'

'Oh Christ . . .'

'I'm sorry. We did what we could.'

'Thanks. Appreciate it.'

'Got chucked about, didn't she? No seat-belt.'

'I did warn her.'

'Friend of yours, or . . .?'

'Just a friend, that's right. We'd been for a couple of drinks. I reckoned I was okay to drive, but we got in the slipstream of this truck . . .'

'We'll be needing a sample from you. Blood or urine.'

'I understand. God, what a mess.'

The officer led him across to the ambulance. Once inside, and left to himself for the moment, Dave released a lungful of pent-up breath, allowed his facial muscles to relax in a brief smile.

CHAPTER 11

Anita's first customer of the day, a wash-and-set, was an elderly undemanding lady with, nevertheless, a sharp tongue. While Anita was wrestling with the drenched strands, the head of Detective-Sergeant Bennett appeared at the salon doorway. Spotting her, he came over.

'Never recognized you, for a moment,' he remarked. 'It's the smock. Time for a quick word?'

Anita stopped. 'Back with you in a little while, Mrs Fairbrother. All right?'

'What's that, Anita?'

'I've just got to attend to this gentleman.'

The customer's small face, like a sun-flushed plum, came up and swung about to examine the newcomer. 'Doesn't look as if he needs a haircut,' she observed.

'He's not here for a haircut.'

'What's he after, then?'

'Shan't keep you long. Don't touch your curlers.'

Sergeant Bennett was gazing spellbound at the sight of a youthful client who was receiving a nouveau-punk treatment from Selina Hodges, the acknowledged expert in the field. Anita said, 'Want to keep watching? Or shall we go into the rest-room?'

'Not much gen for you, I'm afraid,' said Bennett, following her into the cubicle where the junior made tea and coffee. 'Just called round to bring you up to date. We've not had a break, yet. That's really what it amounts to. In a case of this sort—'

'You mean nobody's come forward to say, Yes, I saw this character lurking in the neighbourhood about that time: he had ginger hair and a tattoo down one cheek?'

'Something like that,' admitted the sergeant, taking her half-seriously, 'would be a big help. What I really have in mind, though, is some kind of follow-up offence that might give us a lead on the initial one. You follow?'

'Yes, I'm not that thick. If you ran in somebody who'd just committed a robbery, and his fingerprints matched the ones you found in my great-aunt's house . . .'

'Something very much along those lines. It's our best hope, frankly.'

'What if he lies low for the next six months?'

'He might, of course.'

'And meanwhile, the trail goes cold?'

Bennett shook his head. 'Makes no difference. We could still pin it on him.'

Anita stared down at the electric kettle. 'I want results sooner than that.'

'Don't we all, Miss Blythe? Sadly, in a case like this—'

'You keep on using that expression. Aren't most cases like this?'

'To tell you the honest truth,' Bennett said with confiding forbearance, 'a lot of them, as you say, are apt to be along similar lines. Patience is what's needed. We just have to wait for the culprit to play into our hands. Which a remarkable number of them in fact do, sooner or later.'

'What of all this technology you're always bragging about?'

'It can only achieve so much, you know. It's a bit like a computer. Marvellous gadget, but unless it has data to chew on it's up the creek without a motor. Same goes for the hi-tech forensic stuff. Okay, we can match print with print, hair with hair, blood group with blood group . . . but what we can't do is produce the matching subject out of thin air, so to speak. We have to stick around till he shows himself. Then we're in business.'

Hands in smock pockets, Anita leaned against the wall. 'Presumably, then, the prints you got from the house aren't on file?'

'You've got it. Either he's a bungling teenager who went berserk on his first job, or he's a pro who's so far managed to stay clear of us, kept a clean sheet. They're the worst. Until we catch up with them, they're always one step ahead.'

'Or several steps?' she suggested.

'Possibly.'

'So what it boils down to,' Anita said after an interval, 'is that you're going to mark time until the next atrocity occurs? And then hope to grab the offender for both crimes?'

Sergeant Bennett looked at her, deadpan. 'Do you have a better suggestion, Miss Blythe?'

'You're not interested in my suggestions.'

'You mustn't think that. We don't resent help from the public, I can assure you. On the contrary, we beg for it. Owing to manpower problems, the quantity of routine investigation we can undertake—'

'Isn't this tantamount to just handing it to the criminal on a plate?'

The sergeant heaved breath into his lungs. 'If local residents,' he said weightily, 'were more inclined to take note of what goes on in their neighbours' homes and gardens, sooner than pack themselves away in front of their TVs and block out the real world, we'd be getting places. We might pick up some useful information, instead of—'

'You're asking people to snoop?'

'A spot of neighbourly nosiness might have done your aunt no harm, might it?' The sergeant paused. '*Prior* to the event, as well as during it.'

'Is that meant as a dig at me?'

'By no means. I'm certain you did all you could for her.'

'Well, you're wrong. I didn't.'

He surveyed her. 'So, now you're set on making amends for what you see as your neglect?'

'Call it what you like.' Anita gave the kettle a shove with her hand, sliding it across the table.

'I can understand how you feel,' said Sergeant Bennett, after a space. 'When something like this occurs, obviously the tendency is to start blaming oneself for what one failed to do beforehand. But try to think positively. You were round there, weren't you, twice in two days? You reported your concern to me. The fact that we were just too late to prevent a tragedy is nobody's fault—except the culprit's. Keep that in mind, Miss Blythe, and you'll finish up with a better perspective. Meanwhile . . .'

'You'll sit around waiting for another six-stone nona-
genarian to be killed, in the hope that it might help?'

'I somewhat doubt,' he said with restraint, 'whether we'll
be doing a lot of sitting. We do have various other matters
to attend to, as it happens. And we are overstretched. But
that's our problem, not yours.'

'Sorry. I'm sure you're doing all you humanly can.'

'By the bye,' he added from the door, 'if you should want
to call in at your aunt's house, they've finished with it now.
Picked up all the . . . er . . . traces they're likely to. You
hold a key, I believe?'

'Yes. I borrowed it from her on Sunday.'

He nodded and went out. In a moment he was back. 'If,
by chance, you stumble on something we've missed . . . let
us know about it, won't you? Don't hug it to yourself.'

In addition to the chilled atmosphere, the hall seemed to
echo in a way that it hadn't when Auntie Maisie was alive
and living there. Could one small human body absorb so
many vibrations? Shivering, Anita went through to the
living-room, by-passing the kitchen door which was shut.

Already, after a few days, the furniture looked as if it were
being held in store, waiting for auction. Some of it, she
noted, occupied different positions. The forensic team had
evidently been thorough. A compound of indefinable odours
hung in the air.

She was glad, after all, that she had come alone. But for
Steve's duty flight to Barbados, she would have been
tempted to accept his offer to accompany her, which might
not have been such a good idea. His presence, while helpful
in one sense, would have distracted her. This way, she could
bring concentration to bear.

Fragments of one pane of the french window still lay
scattered about the carpet. The door itself had been secured
with a length of wood screwed to the frame. Trying to keep

her mind relatively blank, Anita embarked on a disciplined
tour of the room, alert for any changes—other than pos-
itional ones—since her previous visit. Few were apparent.
Whatever technology had been employed, such as dusting
powder for fingerprints, its residue had been removed, leaving everything in clean and sterile condition, like a fish-slab.
Pausing at the table, Anita sat down and had a little weep.

Presently she went upstairs. This was something she had
never done while Auntie Maisie was alive. The state of the
first floor came as something of a shock to her. Manifestly,
it had been left for years as a monument to Great-Uncle
Eric, the remote figure last seen by Anita on the occasion of
his retirement from the local authority's Parks Department,
when 'a few drinks' had been arranged in celebration. Anita,
a child at the time, could barely recall his face. But she had
a distinct memory of her great-aunt's, flushed and eager,
thrilled by the prospect of having her Eric at home with her
on a permanent basis. The new phase of their life had
endured for just sixteen months. Then, Great-Uncle Eric
had succumbed without fuss to his chronic bronchitis; and
after that, for his small indomitable widow, the route had
been rockier by the mile.

Three of the bedrooms were empty: the fourth contained
the beds and other furniture from all of them, heaped at
random around the walls, some of it standing in puddles of
its own powder from woodworm borings. Such carpeting as
survived was dropping to pieces. The rest of the flooring
consisted of crazed linoleum of a peculiar mint green which
contributed strongly to the general effect of decay. Over-
whelmed by depression, Anita mounted to the attic floor.

Here, two further bedrooms led off from a small landing,
the ceiling of which housed a trapdoor to the loft. On this
floor, the solitary article of furniture was an ancient chest
of drawers against the landing wall: apart from one of the
wrought-iron handles which had come adrift, its drawers

were void. On top of it, however, lay a kind of steel bolt with a knurled knob at one end. Eyeing the trapdoor speculatively, Anita dragged the chest to a position beneath it, climbed up, inserted the bolt in a hole at one side. A twist released a catch, and she was then able to lift the trapdoor, revealing utter darkness and a stench of damp timber. Shuddering, she lowered the trapdoor hastily and jumped down.

Leaving the chest where it was, she returned downstairs, came to an indecisive standstill in the hall.

Auntie Maisie, it was clear, had made no use of the upper floors for half a decade or more. At the end of the hall was a cloakroom that she had made use of, cutting out the need for expeditions to the upstairs bathroom. To Anita's knowledge, she had always kept herself clean. She was scrupulous about that, and her attire, which she had invariably washed by hand to dry on a wooden clothes-horse in front of an oil fire in the living-room. All this tedious work she had taken for granted. 'It's what I'm used to, dear,' she had once told Anita, aghast at the mere notion of a washing machine with its 'electrics' and its 'programmes'. Plenty of hot water, she had explained, and some soap powder were all she needed. 'If I can't wring, I just let it drip over the hearth. Soon dries out.'

With an involuntary shake of the head, Anita forced herself along to the kitchen door, clasped the handle, let herself through.

The fish-slab approach had been applied here, too. Everything was in place. Instinctively raising her feet over the place on the floor where Auntie Maisie had been lying, Anita went with deliberate purposefulness to the worktop drawers and tugged them out in sequence. Their contents ranged from cutlery to headscarves. Old kid gloves were there in quantity. Spectacles in cases, several pairs of them. Receipts for household bills. Junk mail.

Rummaging through it all, Anita found nothing of significance. The same went for the decrepit wall-cupboards and the varnished dresser: these held mainly tins of soup and pet food, along with dog meal, dog biscuits, dog sprays and other canine provisions, including conditioning powders, ear drops and insecticidal shampoos. Closing the doors on them, she stood back and ran a hand slowly through her hair.

The larder door caught her eye. Behind it, she discovered a broom, a carpet sweeper of vintage design, a biscuit tin full of dusters and wax polish, and a large can of paraffin for the oil fire. It was nearly full. The rest of the storage space seemed to have been unused, unless the police had cleared it out for exploratory purposes, and there was no sign of that.

Returning to the hall, Anita tried the door of the room at the front of the house to which Auntie Maisie had always referred as 'the parlour'. As with the bedrooms, its interior spoke loudly of disuse. Dust-sheets covered the dining table and six chairs, and there was a general sense of clammy airlessness. The sole other piece of furniture was a bureau-cum-bookcase of chipped mahogany with a foot missing: the deprived leg was propped on a volume of poems by Tennyson. Apart from a few lead pencils, a pile of old greetings cards and a tin of assorted buttons, the shelves and cubbyholes of the artefact were empty. Closing it up, Anita quitted the room thankfully and returned once more to the living-room.

The mantelpiece, to which she now turned her attention, held in addition to the clock a number of items both decorative and functional: vases, bowls, tiny boxes in polished veneers. Inside them she found a thimble, hairgrips, empty cotton reels, more pencils, and an abundance of dust. Five minutes was enough to complete the search. Turning away, she tried the table. It was the plainest of pieces, a top and four legs, with a single drawer at one end, so stiff that she could barely wrench it open. When it finally yielded, it proved to hold only a set of place-mats, heavily stained, decorated with hunting scenes. Thrusting it back, Anita turned once more to gaze speculatively at Auntie Maisie's armchair.

As a child, she had once or twice been permitted to occupy it herself. Its contours had always fascinated her. The wings and backrest were so fashioned that it seemed they had been intended for quite another chair, but for some reason had been pressed into use for this one and attached in a loose, slipshod manner with improvised screws and nuts. On the undercarriage, however, some ingenuity had been expended. Beneath the upholstery, a sliding mechanism enabled its shape to be adjusted by vigorous movement of the incumbent body, albeit the consequent alteration of posture could seldom be forecast with reliability. Anita had enjoyed experimenting. On one memorable occasion she had succeeded in dismembering most of the working parts; thereafter, she had faced a strict ban on further use of the contraption.

Partly for this reason, she found herself reluctant to go near it again. Overcoming her hesitancy, she lifted the cushions to expose the substructure, a tangle of wood, metal and padding which looked as though it had been thrown together by a taxidermist in a temper, with total disregard for symmetry or style. The fact that it was unpolluted by biscuit crumbs or more pencils suggested that the police forensic team had not omitted it from their search. Experimentally, however, Anita inserted her fingers into the gap.

The hidden gap. The one she remembered clearly from her childhood: the elasticated hollow between padded base and side panel that had a habit of opening and closing itself according to the adjustments made to the chair. Several times, in her youthful experience, an exciting find like a dropped coin or a squashed toffee had yielded itself to the questing touch. This time, the gap was empty.

There was however an edge of material, slightly stiffer than its immediate surroundings, which lifted as her finger-tips probed. Moving her wrist along, she clamped the edge with finger and thumb, pulled cautiously. The article that emerged was postcard-sized, royal blue, housed in a clear plastic holder. It was a building society passbook.

The town centre branch was active when she arrived. Joining the queue, she waited eight minutes for a till to become vacant. The teller behind it was a large, lumpish girl with a discontented expression who gave Anita the merest wisp of a smile. Sliding the passbook under the glass screen, Anita said, 'I'd like to speak to the cashier who paid out on those last two transactions. Is that possible?'

The girl studied the entries in silence. Eventually she looked up. 'Are they wrong, then?'

'I shouldn't think so. I just want a word with whoever dealt with them.'

The girl pursed her heavily inflated lips. 'No way of checking. It's all done on the computer, see?'

'I know. But you'll have noticed that both those last amounts were withdrawn on the same day. That's a bit unusual, surely? I thought it might have stuck in someone's mind.'

'Not in mine, sorry. Can't you remember who you had?'

'It's not my account. I'm inquiring on the investor's behalf.'

'Mrs M. Holwood . . . Elm Chase.' The dull eyes of the cashier came up again. 'Does she have some complaint? Shouldn't the money have been paid out?'

'I'm sure there's been no mistake on your part. It's just

that some confusion has arisen and I'd like to get it sorted out.'

'You could try asking along.' The girl indicated her colleagues with half a nod. 'One of them might remember. Tag on behind that next customer, there.'

Feeling conspicuous, Anita stationed herself at the out-thrust elbow of a bulky man who was talking earnestly through the glass at the next till. The cashier dealing with him was physically in direct contrast with her neighbour: dark-haired, with a small, pointed face, she wore spectacles with fancy frames that gave her, with apparent injustice, the appearance of a dumb brunette. From her replies to the customer, Anita inferred that she did not lack intelligence. When at last the man moved away, Anita moved smartly into his place, aimed her best smile at the brunette. 'I'm afraid I'm another one with a query.'

She received a quick answering beam. 'That's what we're here for. How can I help?'

Heartened, Anita showed her the passbook. Examining the final entries, the brunette said nothing for a moment; then she glanced up to eye Anita with a hint of curiosity. 'Yes . . . I do remember Mrs Holwood coming in.'

Anita's heart skipped. 'I hoped somebody might.'

'Normally I doubt if I would. But it was a little unusual . . .' The cashier hesitated. 'Excuse my asking, but are you a friend of Mrs Holwood's?'

'A relative. Actually, she's just died.'

'Oh dear. I am sorry.'

'To be exact, she was killed. An intruder broke into her house.'

The brunette stared through the screen. 'Not the old lady at the weekend? I read about it. How awful. A relation of yours? That's really terrible. It was all over the front page of the local. I must have seen the name, only I never made the connection at the time. Dear me. You must be feeling so angry . . .' She paused. 'We're not meant to discuss customer accounts,' she said guardedly, 'with anybody else at all—not unless it's the police, or—'

'I'm making inquiries on behalf of the police,' Anita said fluently. 'They're a bit stretched for manpower, so they asked me if I'd mind calling in and trying to trace the cashier my great-aunt dealt with. It's those last two withdrawals, of course, we're interested in. Both on the same day. Is there anything you can tell me about them?'

'I can't see there'd be any harm . . .' Reaching a decision, the girl leaned forward, lowered her voice to the point of inaudibility. 'It did strike me as a bit funny, to be honest. First time she came in, she took out two hundred and fifty in cash—that's our limit, in one day—and asked for another five hundred by cheque, made payable to someone else. Who was it, now? Somebody Irish.'

'Irish?'

'An Irish name. I'll think of it in a minute. Anyway, I did that for her and she left. Then an hour or so later, back she came again. This time she wanted to draw a cheque for six thousand, payable to the same person. That's why it lodged in my mind. It seemed such an odd way of doing things.'

'Did she seem upset?'

The girl pondered. 'The first time, she was a bit uptight and confused, as though she wasn't used to over-the-counter transactions with us . . . but not upset, no. The second time . . .'

'How would you describe her behaviour?' Anita prompted, as the girl paused again.

'Rather tense. Apprehensive.'

Anita nodded slowly. 'Did you query the second withdrawal?'

'I think I said something to her about having changed her mind—in case she'd genuinely forgotten, you know,

being a bit elderly—but all she said was that another
expense had cropped up and she needed the money, so there
wasn't much else I could do. I did go to the back and
mention it to the assistant manager, Mr Revis, but he
couldn't see any reason to delay payment. As it took the
account to below five hundred, though, and a lower rate of
interest, he suggested I point that out to her. Which I did.'

'What did she say to that?'

'Nothing, really. I'm not sure that it sank in. She just
took the cheque and left again.'

'By herself?'

'No,' the girl said significantly. 'Somebody was waiting
for her.'

'A man?'

'Right. A slim bloke, sort of middle-aged, quite nattily
dressed . . . a bit of a dandy, in fact. Wavy fair hair. They
swapped a word or two at one of the tables over there: then
he took her by the arm and they went out. I noticed,' the
cashier added defensively, 'because by that time I was taking
more interest in Mrs Holwood than I generally would in a
customer, after dealing with them, so I kept an eye on her
for a few seconds. Once she'd left, though, she went right
out of my mind. Until now.'

Anita glanced round. The queue behind her was starting
to look restive. 'One other thing,' she said quietly. 'Was the
same man with her the first time, did you happen to notice?'

'That's what I can't be sure about. I've a feeling he might
have been, but I couldn't swear to it. I just have this idea,
looking back, that someone did meet her at the door on the
first occasion. I could be wrong.'

'Wrong or not, you've been very helpful.' Anita took back
the passbook. 'Thanks a lot.'

'Should I tell the police about it?' the girl asked anxiously.
'Or will you be—'

'Don't you bother. I'll make sure they get to hear.'

CHAPTER 12

Percy was clasping a pint of bitter at the bar and looking preoccupied. At Nigel's appearance he thrust the tankard aside and grabbed him by an arm.

'What's been keeping you? Did you talk to Dave?'

'I did not.' Disengaging his sleeve, Nigel signalled to Frankie the barman.

'Why the bleeding heck not?'

'Because I can't find him. The usual, Frankie, thank you kindly. I've been round to all the obvious places,' Nigel continued, unbuttoning his new Harris tweed jacket and smoothing down his cravat, 'and as a last resort I asked at Tracy's, in case he'd gone back to *her*; in addition to which, I've left word at various other locations for him to call me, which to date he hasn't, unless . . . Any messages for me, Frankie, since yesterday?'

'Not a tweet, Mr Murphy. There you go, sir. One-eighty, to you.'

'In healthier times,' Nigel told him, sliding a note across, 'I'd ask you to keep the change. But times are a little below par, just now.'

'Sorry to hear that, sir.'

'Me too,' muttered Percy, nudging Nigel aside. 'What's all this, then—below par? I thought we was sitting pretty. What happened to the doings?'

'I'm just creating a good impression,' Nigel explained. 'We wouldn't want anyone getting the idea we were loaded at the moment, would we?'

'You might be right.' Percy still looked troubled. 'So, when's the payout?'

'I'm deferring it.'

'Wotcha mean, you're deferring it?'

'I mean I'm taking no chances. If I were to walk into my bank this afternoon,' Nigel enlarged, sipping delicately from his glass, 'and draw a couple of thousand smackers in ready cash, don't you think it's just possible I might call a bit of attention to myself? At this stage of proceedings, that's the last thing we want.'

'You can say that again.' Returning to the bar for his beer, Percy carried it over and spoke on a lower note than ever. 'All I'm saying is, I could do with a spot of the ready, tide us over, like. Why can't you—'

'Let it ride for a bit. I know what I'm doing.'

'I'm skint.'

Nigel felt for his wallet. 'Twenty any help?'

'You can't be serious.'

'Thirty. What do you have to spend it on, Perce, for Heaven's sake? That plywood hutch on wheels you live in —what does that cost you a week?'

'I've got certain commitments,' Percy explained with dignity. 'Anyway, you owe us a grand. How about ten per cent on account?'

'I don't have that kind of money.'

Percy sniffed. 'Got yourself a nice new jacket, I notice. Never cost you half a quid, if I'm any judge.'

A sigh came from Nigel. 'Let it ride for another twenty-four hours. That's all I ask. Once I've talked to Dave, we can plan accordingly. He might be able to give us the all-clear.'

'And he might not.' Percy gnawed at a fingernail, glancing restlessly about the saloon as if half-expecting uniformed men to start emerging from hidden doors. He edged closer to his associate. 'Between you and me, Nige, I reckon it was him.'

'If it was, he's dropped us well and truly in it.'

Upending his glass, Nigel drained its contents in an

uncharacteristic surge and disposed of it on a shelf holding
a potted plant. He drew Percy into a recess between empty
tables. 'As a matter of interest, what makes you so sure?'

'I know Dave. He's got a temper. Once he loses his cool,
there's no holding him. He might regret it afterwards . . .
and there again, he might not. If you want my honest
opinion, he can be dangerous to know.'

'Now he tells me,' Nigel said bitterly, rubbing his chin.
'What did you want to get linked up with him for, if he's
that undesirable?'

'Never knew he was, did I, till I got to know him?' Percy
was aggrieved. 'You can't pick and choose your mates, to
that extent. He seemed like a good bloke . . . did his bit on
the physical side an' that. But he's got one big fault, I
reckon.'

'And what's that?'

'He's greedy. Doesn't know when to stop.'

'And you feel he didn't stop in time where the old lady
was concerned?'

'Stands to reason, don't it? He said he was going back
there to try his luck. He'd halfway convinced himself she
kept a bunch of readies in the house. So, if he couldn't find
'em, and she wouldn't tell him where they was . . .'

'You may very well be right,' Nigel agreed, with a detect-
able shudder. 'Question is, what are we going to do about
it?'

Percy glanced furtively out of the recess. 'We could shop
him to the Fuzz.'

'I don't know about that.'

'Violence ain't my cup of tea.'

'Mine neither. I'm not thinking of that aspect. What
concerns me, Perce, is that like it or not we're involved in
this, to some degree. Think about it. Even if it wasn't Dave
but someone else—which is stretching the imagination a
few inches—we had dealings with the old biddy just a day

or so beforehand, which frankly puts us in a somewhat fragile position. And if it *was* Dave, it's worse. Suppose he's caught. He's not exactly bonded to us by ties of loyalty: he'll have no hesitation in saying we were all in it. Accessories, Perce. Accessories to murder. That's the situation we'd find ourselves in.'

Percy's thin shoulders sagged. 'You're right,' he muttered despairingly. 'Just what I've been telling meself, all morning.'

'We could deny any part in it, but who'd believe us?'

'Ain't fair. There's no justice.'

'Sometimes, Perce, you have to make your own justice.' Nigel gave his partner a rallying cuff on the upper arm. 'Leave it with me, for the moment. The prime essential is to have a word with friend Dave, face to face, get matters straight before us prior to deciding what to do next. I'll go on looking for him.'

'Yeah, right. And you'll keep us in touch?'

'Don't worry. When I do catch up with him, I'll be needing you.'

The yapping in the outhouse had persisted for an hour before the tolerance of the next-door neighbour finally fell apart and she came round to knock on Vanessa's door.

'I know you're only looking after it for Dave, love, but when's he going to have it back himself? Does he know it's driving us all bonkers?'

'It's only in bursts,' Vanessa protested, in stout defence of her position. 'Exercise is what he wants.'

'Give it some, then. For God's sake.'

'When I've got the time and the energy. Dave's meant to be doing it.'

'So why isn't he?'

'If I had the chance, I'd ask him. Not seen him for five days.'

'Faded out on you, has he?'

'He goes off on jobs. Him and Nigel and that little squirt Percy—they're apt to fetch up the far side of Brum sometimes, mending some roof or other . . . and then they stop away nights as well. He'll show up again in a day or so.'

'When he does, tell him to park that pooch on somebody else, will you? Before we all get perforated eardrums.'

'It's not that bad.' Solidarity with her brother outweighed Vanessa's own mounting exasperation. 'You get more noise from the juggernauts down West Street.'

'That's a different *sort* of noise. Listen, he's off again. Goes right through your head.'

'Tell you what, Doreen. I'll take him round the block, then when we get back I'll give him his dinner with half a tranquillizer in it, same as I did Tuesday. The chemist said it wouldn't hurt him. Keeps him quiet most of the day.'

'What beats me,' grumbled her neighbour, 'is why Dave wanted the dog in the first place, if all he's going to do is leave it here and have it drugged senseless. Daft, I call it.'

'It was straying,' Vanessa explained, 'in the main road. If Dave hadn't picked it up it could have caused an accident.'

'Why didn't he take it to the police?'

'He thought he could give it a home.'

Doreen tossed her head. 'His sister could, you mean. Now you're stuck with the little pest, Van, I reckon. We all are.'

Having closed the door on her irritable friend, Vanessa returned to the scullery and became irritable herself. What did Dave think he was playing at? It was true, what Doreen had said. The ear-splitting Yorkie had been unceremoni-ously dumped on her while Dave breezed off to vanish in the suburbs. At this rate, she'd have some bloke in uniform handing her a summons on the doorstep for disturbing the peace. It wasn't good enough.

On the other hand, she couldn't let her brother down.

She never had. The affinity between them was something that it would have taken more than a stray dog to disintegrate. If Dave had taken a shine to the little creature, there was no more to be said. Not by Vanessa, at least.

In any case, there was always Dave's temperament to be considered. Highly strung, he was: volatile. She had tried crossing him, once or twice, and the experience had not been enjoyable.

With a sigh, Vanessa buckled on her outdoor shoes and went from the scullery to the outhouse with the miniature collar and lead she had picked up at the Bargain Shop.

Returning from his Barbados trip on the Friday evening, Steve entered his flat as the telephone started to burble. Travel-dazed, thirsting for coffee, he groped for the receiver.

'Oh—hi, Anita. Yes, this very second. Quite good, thanks. Any news?'

'I think I might be on to something.' She sounded taut but animated. 'Come up and I'll tell you.'

'I'm a bit . . .' He stopped himself. 'Can I sort myself out a little, first? Be with you in half an hour.'

'Okay. See you then.'

For a few moments he loitered by the phone, scratching his head vacantly. Presently, with a shrug, he transferred his suitcase from floor to sofa, drank some cold water from the tap, left the flat and went upstairs. Anita replied instantly to his ring. Her eyes were bright, her face was slightly flushed. Kissing him lightly on the mouth, she grabbed his hand and towed him through to the living-room.

'So you had a good flight?' Not waiting for an answer, she steamed on immediately. 'I've got a lead on Auntie Maisie's killer, you'll be glad to hear.'

'Terrific!' Steve pondered her. '*You* have? Or the cops?'

'As yet, they don't come into it.' She made a dismissive gesture. 'I'm following it up myself.'

'Watch your step, love, I should. You're dealing with . . .
Listen, you weren't thinking of making coffee, by any
chance?'

'Are you desperate for a fix? Come into the kitchen. I can
be telling you while it's brewing. There's something I want
your advice on.'

Listening intently to her account, Steve made the coffee
for the pair of them and they drank it at the kitchen
breakfast-bar. Anita seemed almost unaware of what she
was swallowing. Clearly, the bulk of her attention was with
what she had to relate, which she delivered in a series
of quick, excitable phrases that suggested an underlying
motivating force of charged particles. Trying to introduce a
calmer note, Steve sat nodding for a while.

'You seem to have done pretty well. Quite the amateur
sleuth.'

'It's no good, unless I can chase it through to a result.'

'What do the cops say?'

'Nothing.'

'Surely they've made some comment?'

'I've not mentioned it to them,' she said simply.

He stared at her. 'Don't you think you should?'

'What's the point? They haven't the manpower to cope
with half the cases they've got on hand already. Sergeant
Bennett said so himself.'

'Just the same . . . You can't keep this sort of information
from them, Anita. They must know.'

'Why?' she demanded. 'What's the use of passing things
on to them, if they just sit on them? If I take action myself,
at least I know something's being done.'

'Yes, but . . .' Steve fumbled for words. 'They do have
resources that you lack. They've got the experience. Besides
which, I'm not sure you aren't breaking the law, withholding
data like this.'

'Personally,' she said with a touch of contempt, 'I don't

give a fig, right this minute, for anything to do with the law. My one concern is to find the monster who did that to Auntie Maisie. Don't you feel that way?'

'Naturally, but . . . I do feel, love, you should report it. Bring in as much help as you can.'

Anita glanced down at her lap. 'It's you I'm counting on for help.'

'I'll do whatever's possible,' he assured her. 'What did you have in mind?'

She returned to him with animation restored. 'You've contacts, haven't you, with the Press?'

'A few,' he said cautiously, 'from my hack reporter days. But I'm hardly—'

'Could you get something printed in one or two of the papers?'

'I don't know. What kind of thing?'

'A story about Auntie Maisie. The sort they publish sometimes after an attack on an old lady . . . background, lifestyle, you know the type of thing. If you suggested it to one of the tabloids, say?'

'They might bite. But what's the object?' He studied her suspiciously. 'Anita, you're not thinking of trying to lure the killer out of hiding, by some means?'

'That's just what I'm aiming to do.'

'How?'

'By implying in the article that Auntie Maisie really did have a hoard of money stashed away and that it's probably still there. Might give the original intruder food for thought, mightn't it?'

'Damn well might. To say nothing of every other petty housebreaker in the Midlands, each of whom would proceed to home in on Elm Chase like a Cruise missile, cosh and jemmy at the ready. The idea's crazy, Anita. You'd need to set up a rota system to accommodate them all.'

She shook her head mulishly. 'I doubt if anything like

that would happen. Other villains would fight shy. They wouldn't want to run the risk of being mixed up in a case like that.'

'Neither would the real culprit. Having got away with it the first time, he'd hardly be likely—'

'You forget: he's greedy. And having got away with the initial crime, as you say, he might feel tempted to cash in on it. At the moment, he's come away empty-handed. That could be niggling at him.'

'I don't doubt it,' Steve said sardonically. 'Causing him no end of regret, that's for sure. But I still question whether he'd be insane enough to rise to as obvious a bait as that.'

'It needn't be obvious. The bit about the money could be subtly worked in.'

'Who by?'

Anita sat looking at him. He puffed out both cheeks. 'You've an inflated notion of my skills as a wordsmith; not to mention my influence with the tabloid nationals. The only thing I might be able to do . . .'

'Yes?' she urged.

'The news editor of the *Scanner* is a mate of mine,' Steve said reluctantly. 'At least he was, last time we met. I stood him drinks then, so I guess he owes me. Oh, and I wangled him a cut-price fortnight in the Canaries. He might not have forgotten.'

'There you are, then! The *Scanner* would be ideal. It covers the whole of this area. Can you do it for me?'

'I'll give it a bash. Can't promise anything. Hold on a bit though, Anita. Suppose, just suppose, this imbecile lure happens to work. The culprit ventures back for another search of the premises . . . but when? He might wait several weeks. Are the cops going to be agreeable to staking the place out all that time?'

'We won't rely on the police.'

'We won't?'

'No. I thought, if you and I took turns to sleep at the—'

Steve leapt up. 'Now I've heard everything. That really takes the banana. Have you any idea, Anita, what you're suggesting? The risks involved? Aside from which, when do either of us make up on our lost sleep? If I'm between trips, I might bear up under the stress, but you have to be at the salon every morning at—'

'Not any more I don't.'

'Huh?'

'I quit.'

'You what?'

'I wanted time to myself,' she explained calmly, 'so that I could concentrate on this. So I handed in my notice.'

Steve billowed his cheeks again. 'And how do you reckon to live?'

'Once this is over, I can get another job elsewhere. Hair stylists are always in demand.'

'Maybe, but there seem to be an awful lot of you. What if you found yourself—'

'If it came to the worst,' Anita said wearily, 'I could always take on customers at home. I'm not bothered about it. I have some money saved up. And another thing—I'm told I shall inherit Auntie Maisie's house, as next of kin. So I'm not going to be destitute, am I?'

'Quite the reverse,' Steve acknowledged, impressed. 'Even as it stands, that place must be worth a small fortune. And if the site was sold for redevelopment . . .'

'I can't think about it at the moment. What matters to me is nailing this barbarian.'

'Don't let it become an obsession.'

She looked back at him. 'It already has,' she said quietly. 'I want it that way.' There was a brief pause. 'Will you try the *Scanner* with that article?' she asked.

He flung out a hand. 'For you, Anita, I'll trade my soul. But on one condition.'

'Which is?'

'That we bring the police in on it, right from the start. Otherwise it's too chancy.'

Anita pondered for a moment. 'Okay,' she said lightly. 'I'll speak to Chief Inspector Davison or someone about it. That satisfy you?'

He eyed her narrowly. 'I guess so. You'll talk to him in the morning?'

'You've got a deal.' Rising, Anita advanced across the room to slide into the embrace of his outstretched arms. 'Did I mention, Steve, it's nice to see you back?'

'In point of fact, no, but I was egotistical enough to take it as read.' For a minute or so they remained locked silently together, their foreheads touching. 'You're softer than you look,' he remarked, squeezing her ribs. 'Not nearly as bony as the casual observer might assume.'

'Thanks. Will you promise me something?'

'Haven't I already?'

'On a personal basis. When we've got time to play around, will you let me have a go at your hair?'

'Why? What's wrong with it?'

'Where do you want me to start?'

'You're very nearly as insulting as I am,' he remarked. 'Okay, I'll be your first home client, if you insist. By then, you may need the money.'

'It'll be on the house.' Uncrossing her eyes from an inspection of his scalp, Anita smiled up at him. 'Auntie Maisie,' she said softly, 'would have enjoyed seeing us together. Let's do what we can for her, right? The pair of us.'

CHAPTER 13

'I've not clapped eyes on him,' declared Vanessa, wiping pastry crumbs off her fingers. 'Not since you asked us last time. I thought he was with you.'

'What gave you that idea?' Nigel asked politely.

'Well, he generally is, when he goes off. You work together, don't you?' Vanessa hadn't much time for Nigel. An overdressed smoothie, she considered him, with an out-size opinion of himself. And a faintly creepy side to his personality, into the bargain. Nothing she could pin down, but . . . 'That's what Dave's given us to understand, any-how,' she added, wondering if she could wriggle out of offering her unwelcome visitor a cup of tea.

Nigel treated her to one of his smiles. 'You mustn't believe all you hear from Dave.'

'I'm to mistrust my own brother, you mean?'

Nigel shrugged. 'You know him better than I do,' he said ambiguously. 'I'm sorry to have troubled you unnecessarily. I did think he might be staying here.'

'Is it some job you want him for?'

'In a manner of speaking.'

'What's that supposed to mean?'

'We've a proposition for him. Percy and I. Will you tell him that, Vanessa, when he does get in touch?'

'If he does.'

Nigel raised his eyebrows. 'Sooner or later he's bound to show up. Who's that regular of his, what's her name—Tracy, over in Coventry? I gave her a buzz, two days ago, but she said she hadn't seen him for weeks. You've not spoken to her, by any chance, since then?'

'I've more to do with my time,' Vanessa retorted, 'than

waste it nattering with Dave's girlfriends. Look, I must get round to the shops. If Dave calls in, I'll let you know, Nigel. All right?'

'No need for you to bother. Just tell him I'd like to see him.'

'Does he know where to—'

'Usual place. We've only . . .' Nigel paused. A shrill noise was coming from the back of the house. 'Hallo-allo. Wasn't aware you kept pets.'

Vanessa snorted. 'I don't. I'm looking after it for Dave. One of his impulse pick-ups.'

'Well I never. What is it?'

'One of them little Yorkies, whiskers all round his face. Not my type of dog, to be honest. I'd sooner have something bigger you can get hold of.'

Nigel nodded understandingly. 'Slightly naughty of Dave,' he remarked, 'to swing it on you like that. No wonder he's keeping clear. Mind if I take a look?'

'What for?'

'I'm quite interested in dogs. Might even consider taking it off your hands, if you've had an overdose of the little rascal.'

'He's not mine to give away,' Vanessa pointed out, looking thoughtful just the same. 'Dave might take a dim view.'

'If he kicks up about it, refer him to me.'

'You'd better see for yourself first,' Vanessa suggested with some nervousness. 'You might change your mind.'

She led Nigel through to the scullery, where Ouncey sat indignantly on an old tweed jacket inside a cardboard box in a corner. At their entrance his yap soared to a squeal that ripped at the eardrums. Nigel winced.

'Musical, isn't he? Neighbours putting up with it?'

'They've had a few things to say.'

Nigel stood contemplating the dog. 'How about it then,

Vanessa?' he inquired presently. 'Like me to take it off your hands?'

Vanessa pretended to give it further thought, although her mind was already made up. 'I'd be quite glad if you would, to be honest. What with everything else, I can't really cope at the moment. I'll tell Dave you've got him.'

'Unless I see him first. And if he wants him back,' Nigel said, approaching the animal with caution, 'it's me he'll have to deal with. Here, boy. Come to your Uncle Nigel. Din-dins? Has he eaten yet?'

'Bit of Weetabix for breakfast. He never seems that hungry.'

'Pining for his real owner, maybe. Let's have his collar and leash and I'll pack him in the car.'

'You will look after him?' Vanessa demanded anxiously.

'Five-star comfort,' Nigel promised, securing the collar gingerly about the tiny neck of the Yorkie. 'Rest assured, Vanessa my sweet, he'll be fine with me. I know just how to handle dogs.'

Percy was at the bar, taking hunted pecks at a half-pint of bitter. 'Seen the *Scanner*?' he muttered.

'Gave her a fair old splash, didn't they?'

'You sound mighty relaxed about it. Listen, Nige, I'm not too happy meself. How'd they know about the money? Them first reports, all they said—'

'They don't *know* about any money,' Nigel said soothingly. 'Any more than we do. They're just speculating.'

'No, they ain't. This niece of the old bird's—'

'She was just putting two and two together and making nine, for the sake of a story. She admits she doesn't know where the hoard is. That's tantamount to saying she hasn't a clue whether it exists or not.'

'Far as we're concerned,' Percy muttered, 'it don't make a lot of difference. Dave's queered our pitch, good and proper. Any trace of the young bastard yet?'

'I've just come from his sister's. He's not been in touch. He's keeping low, no doubt about it. Which doesn't bode well, I'm afraid, Perce old chum. Either he did it, which means he's having to stay under cover, or he's afraid they'll think he did it, which in Dave's book means likewise. Whatever the case—'

'If he does finally get himself run in, he'll blow the gaff on the pair of us.'

'All we have to do is say what really happened.'

'And the Fuzz'll believe us? Just like that? You're a bloody optimist.'

'Alternatively . . .'

Percy glanced up as Nigel paused. 'Wha'?'

'We *could* try to ensure,' Nigel murmured abstractedly, 'that he avoids getting himself run in.'

'Oh yeh? And how d'you suggest we do that?'

'Got any suggestions yourself?'

Percy looked blank. 'Tell him to get out of here, down to London or somewhere?'

'What makes you think that would help? He'd be more at risk there, not less. Of course, he may already have done something like that of his own accord, but I somehow doubt it. London's not Dave's scene. No, I'm working on the assumption that he's still around here, in which case . . .' Nigel drifted into reverie.

Percy studied him hopefully. 'Feel an idea coming on, Nige?'

'I may have. Finish your drink and come outside.'

'Where we off to?'

'Just a spin in the car. We can talk better there.'

From the rear seat, the Yorkie greeted them with something between a growl and a gurgle. Nigel had tethered it by its lead to an armrest, and the dog's frustration had boiled up to a pitch that was causing its eyes to bulge in a manner which discouraged Percy from making overtures from the front passenger seat. 'Thought you said you'd not seen Dave?' he queried, eyeing the animal with a certain mystification. 'This is the one, ain't it? The one he took off the old—'

'That's right, the formidable Ouncey himself. Vanessa had him.'

'Since when?'

'Since Day One, I imagine.' Swerving out of the Fiddler's car park, Nigel set course for the town perimeter. 'Apparently Dave just dumped him on her, then faded out.'

'She brassed off about it?'

'The neighbours were. So I kindly offered to take him off her hands.'

'Dave must be crackers. That mutt could put us all inside.'

'Which is the very reason,' Nigel explained, wriggling the car between two lorries and bringing Percy's heart into his throat, 'why he's there on the back seat at this moment. Once I get him home, I'll be attending to him, Perce, don't you worry.'

'Slip something in his dogmeal?'

'Leave the detail to me.'

'I wouldn't waste any time about it. That dog—'

'I know, I know, he's a menace. Don't worry. I'm just as anxious as you are to eliminate the risk. That's my department. Now let's talk about yours.'

'Mine?'

'Back in the pub, we were discussing Dave. Remember?' Percy nodded uneasily. 'So?'

'So I thought you might try dragging a corner of that imagination of yours out of cold storage. Look at it this way, Perce. What we need is decisive action, right? Something to discourage friend Dave from making any unseemly revelations of an incriminating nature involving others besides himself. Do you follow me?'

'I agree with what you're saying,' said Percy, gazing nervously at the road ahead. 'What I don't see is where I come in. You're meant to be the brains around here.'

Nigel sighed elaborately. 'Okay, I'll shoulder the entire workload as usual. Here's the proposition. What we need, first of all, is a job on a nice three- or four-storey property, somewhere quiet . . .

'Don't we always?'

'And it so happens,' Nigel continued, ignoring the interjection, 'that I might have just such a job lined up. It's not in the bag yet, but I'm working on it. That's not the problem. The problem is Dave. Contacting him.'

A frown had established itself on Percy's narrow forehead. 'Suppose we do, and he agrees to come in on the job? How does that help us?'

Roaring the car past a single-decker bus, Nigel returned to top gear and drove into a sharp bend at fifty. 'The way it helps,' he said kindly, 'is by getting the two of you up there together on the roof, in the manner to which you've both become accustomed. That's the first step.'

'Oh yeh?' Percy cleared his throat. 'What's the second?' he demanded hoarsely.

'The second is that Dave experiences a sudden unfortunate attack of vertigo. You know what vertigo is, Perce, don't you? Fear of heights.'

'Dave don't give a bugger about heights. If it was fire . . . Fire sends him paralytic. Heights—'

'Nature can always be given a spot of assistance, Perce. Like a tiny shove at the correct instant. That's all it would take.'

Percy twisted slowly in his seat. 'A shove? Who from?'

Nigel said nothing, but raised his eyebrows.

Agitation seized the posture of the smaller man. 'Now look. This ain't my territory, Nige. No *way*. I'm not getting—'

'You might have no choice, dear boy.'

'Either way, I'm not doing it.'

'All right. I'm listening.'

'Eh?'

'What's your counter-proposal?'

'Why don't we just put the frighteners on him? Tell him . . .'

'Tell him what?'

'You think of something.'

'I've thought of something.'

'It's bloody lunatic, Nige. What if I cocked it up? What if he fell on something soft and picked himself up and—'

'What if he turned into a rag doll and floated off on the breeze? Think positively, Perce. Choose your moment, act decisively and you can't miss.'

'Dave's not here, though, is he?' Percy said desperately. 'Can't do nothing about it if he's not here.'

Nigel said confidently, 'He won't want to keep out of sight indefinitely. He'll be after his cash. And when I tell him he'll have to wait for it, he might flip his lid but he won't dare make an issue of it: he's in no position to, is he? And if I were then to offer him a small but lucrative assignment to tide him over . . .'

'This other job you were talking about?'

'You're catching on.'

'Where abouts is it?'

'Funnily enough, it's not so far from the last one. You remember Elm Chase, of course. Well, running parallel—'

'I'm not going back inside three miles of that place.'

'Running parallel,' Nigel continued with composure, 'is another, similar street by the name of Oak Avenue: while we were in the neighbourhood, in my thrifty fashion I scouted it out. And in one of the houses, a very Victorian edifice indeed, there dwells this elderly courteous gentleman who was most grateful to be told that his roof was about ready to drop off and is expecting a return visit any day now to finalize details of a rescue operation. Now, doesn't that strike you as a remarkable opportunity?'

'What for?'

'What we've just been discussing.'

'You speak for yourself. I ain't discussing nothing.'

For a few moments Nigel concentrated on the road conditions, humming softly to himself. From the back of the car, a sudden shrill yap from Ouncey caused Percy to jump violently, then subside cursing. As they reached a clear stretch of the route, Nigel interrupted his humming to direct a sidelong glance at his companion.

'If it's conscience troubling you, Perce, my advice is to ignore it. You read what happened to the old girl?'

'Don't remind me.' Percy closed his eyes. Reopening them presently, he added, 'I'm not saying I approve of violence. It ain't my scene, Nige, you know that. If it was Dave did that to her, he's got it coming to him, I reckon. Only I'm not the bloke to do the delivering. It ain't down to me. You'll have to find someone—'

'I'm doing my bit,' Nigel remarked on a note of mild reproof. 'I'm seeing to the dog, aren't I? I'd have thought you'd be willing to pitch in and attend to your end. Considering it's in the best interests of both of us.'

Percy sat in silence, holding tight to the door handle as they went through a series of bends. Eventually he cleared his throat again, long and chokily. 'Tell us what you want us to do.'

Having dropped Percy off at his trailer site, with instructions to hold himself available, Nigel put in a call from a roadside Phonecard booth which happened to be in working order. After some delay a female voice replied.

'Nigel Murphy here,' he said courteously.

'Oh yes?'

'Can I speak to Dave?'

'Dave? He's not here.'

'Yes, he is, Doris. He told me he was staying with you.'

'Well, he was putting you on. I've not seen him in weeks.'

'Oh dear, what a pity. If you do see him, perhaps you wouldn't mind mentioning that I've something for him. Something to his advantage.'

A pause ensued. 'What do I tell him it is?'

'I think I'd sooner explain that myself, if you don't mind.'

'If it's anything to do with a job, he's not after one at the moment.'

'How d'you know that, Doris? I thought you said you hadn't seen him.'

Another pause. 'All right, clever clogs. I might have seen him around, but he told me . . .'

'I think I can guess what he told you,' Nigel informed her, ending a third hiatus in the conversation. 'He'll want to hear about this, though, believe me. What a shame he can't come to the telephone. Never mind, it'll have to wait. If and when you do see him again, which as his ex-missus you're quite likely to I assume, you might draw his attention to the—'

'Hang on a bit. I think I heard someone at the back door.'

Wearing a half-smile, Nigel waited. After a medium interval Dave's growl drifted into his left ear. 'What do you want?'

'I want the team to get together,' Nigel told him cheerily. 'We've marked a promising customer and we don't want to lose him.'

'I'm resting.'

'How are the finances, Dave? Keeping our heads above water, are we?'

'I'm not bothered.'

'That doesn't sound like you. The man with a head for

figures. A few extra hundred never did anybody any harm, did they?'

'How about the grand you owe me?'

'Settlement's being deferred, pending clarification of the situation.'

'Look, Murphy, you rat on me and you'll regret it. And another thing—it's *two* grand you owe me. All right? You needn't think—'

'The position's delicate all round, wouldn't you say?' Nigel's half-smile extended itself to the other side of his mouth as he awaited an answer, in vain. 'This other thing,' he resumed finally, 'is different. The proverbial slice of cake. Couple of hours' work, then we're away to share the profits. Are you on?'

'I might be. If the share-out happens.'

'You'll get what's due to you, I'll guarantee.'

He waited again while Dave thought it over. The next question was couched in a tone marginally more conciliatory. 'Where is it, this latest job?'

'Within the immediate district,' Nigel replied smoothly. 'Nice, quiet residential street, detached property, no hassle from neighbours. If you were to meet Perce and me in the van, usual place, first thing in the morning . . .'

'I've not got the van. It's a write-off.'

'Dear me. What have you been up to?'

'Never you mind. If you want me on the job, you'll have to pick me up in your wagon, otherwise it's no deal. And bring your own slates. If it is slates.'

'It's slates. Fair enough, Dave, we'll be there at nine sharp. I think you've made the right decision. See you then.'

Hanging up, Nigel withdrew another Phonecard from his wallet, inserted it, tapped out the communal number at the trailer park. When Percy finally got to the receiver, the Phonecard was expiring rapidly. Nigel made it brief.

'Dave's going to show. Pick you up at eight-thirty. You know what you have to do?'

Percy's voice was thick with apprehension, but compliant. 'I don't like it, Nige. Okay. We've no choice, have we?'

'DANGER' announced the scarlet block lettering on the side of the bottle.

The message beneath, in black, was terse, uncompromising. *The contents of this bottle are poisonous. For gardening use only. NOT to be taken.*

Adding half the compound to the gravy he had prepared in a cup, Nigel poured the mixture over the dogmeat chunks and meal lying in a shallow dish, gave the end-product a good stir, set it down carefully on the floor. 'There you are, fellah. Get stuck into that.'

Quitting the kitchen hastily, he went through to what he called his study. There was an academic streak to Nigel, which he liked to nurture whenever possible. Currently he was studying a book about Black Holes in the cosmos. It was the sort of distraction he urgently needed at the moment. Shutting the door tightly between himself and the kitchen, he fell with a fastidious shudder into his scholarly-looking swivel chair, tilted it back to the maximum angle, grabbed the volume and turned to Part Four: *Inverted Worlds on the Far Side?* Within minutes, the spell of the narrative had captured him. He forgot his surroundings.

Surfacing half an hour later, he sat tensely, listening.

No sound was audible from the kitchen. Placing the book aside, he drew breath, stood, breathed in once more, opened the study door and let himself into the central lobby of the flat. For a moment or two he stood there, muscles braced against squeamishness. When he felt physically under control, he crossed the remainder of the lobby floor, gripped the handle of the kitchen door, threw it open.

From beneath the cooker, Ouncey uttered a low growl, followed by a yap.

'Bloody hell,' murmured Nigel.

He approached the dish. Its contents were untouched. Crouched beside it, he swore elegantly to himself while Ouncey looked on, his eyes protruding. Having worked through his repertoire, Nigel straightened up to collect the spoon from the worktop, stooped again, gave the dogfood a perfunctory follow-up rotation. 'Din-dins, Ouncey,' he coaxed, pushing it closer to the dog. 'Lovely meaty mouthfuls. Try some, you'll love it.'

In a brisk whirl of movement, Ouncey bypassed him and scuttled out of the kitchen.

Nigel cursed again. Lifting the dish, he slapped the food on to several sheets of newspaper, bundled it up, disposed of it in the waste bin. Thoroughly washing his hands, twice, he stood drying them while thinking.

After a while he pulled open a drawer, took out a joint-carver.

The grip was of yellowing bone. The blade, sharp-tipped, had a serrated cutting edge. Placing it on the worktop, he went out to the lobby.

Ouncey had taken refuge under the coatstand. At Nigel's approach he released a falsetto snarl. Flinching slightly, Nigel nevertheless came on, dived, made a grab, pinning the dog to the floor. Despite his squirms and wriggles, Ouncey was helpless as he was borne back to the kitchen and dumped firmly in the sink.

Held down on the stainless steel, the dog launched a faint, whimpering squeal.

With his free hand, Nigel took hold of the carver.

Raising it, point downwards, he hesitated.

The dog looked up at him.

Half an interminable minute elapsed. Abruptly Nigel let go of the carver, which fell with a rattle into the sink. 'Oh

Christ,' he moaned, backing off. 'What do you want to look at me like that for?'

Ouncey sat shivering.

CHAPTER 14

Collecting his mail from the communal table downstairs, Steve spotted Anita's slight figure toiling up the steps from the street. She was holding a small suitcase. He opened the door for her.

'Hi, love. Been out picking mushrooms?'

'Can you do something for me, Steve, later on?'

'As long as it's later.' He glanced at his watch. 'It's seven-fifteen, for God's sake. Did you have a bad night?'

'I've not slept, actually.' Her eyes looked sunken and haunted. 'You're up early as well, though, aren't you? Join the Insomniacs' Club.'

'In my case it's necessity. My editor called me last night with a midday deadline for the Barbados piece, so I'm having to crack on with it. I'm almost through.'

Taking the suitcase from her, he followed her up the stairs. 'What have you got in here—every final edition off the news stand?'

Anita shook her head. 'Just a few oddments from the house.'

'Your Great-Aunt Maisie's? Is that where you've been? I didn't know the buses ran that early.'

'I went round last evening.'

'Spent the night there, you mean?' Grabbing her arm, he arrested her on the first landing. 'I trust you were in the company of a suitably burly police officer, or several?'

'They haven't been assigned yet.'

'What do you mean, haven't been assigned?' He re-

strained her as she started to move off again. 'You spoke
about this to the chief inspector, didn't you?'

'I told you I had.' She avoided looking at him.

'I know you told me. What I'm asking—'

'Don't get heavy, Steve. I'm too tired.'

'Anita, are you telling me you slept alone in that mauso-
leum, waiting for a cold-blooded killer to let himself in from
the garden?'

'I didn't sleep. Coming up for some coffee?'

'And you've not even mentioned any of this to the cops?'
Steve thrust hair despairingly back from his eyes. 'Love,
you're insane. Also deceitful. You gave me a promise. What
is this between you and the law? Some kind of feud?'

'No. I just don't think they're in a position to handle
things properly.'

'Whereas you are?' He stood gazing at her. 'All eight
stone and five feet five of you? Tell me something, I'm
curious. If he had shown up last night, what would you
have done?'

'Called the police.'

'Oh. You'd have gone that far?'

'I'm not entirely impractical,' she said impatiently. She
glanced at the door of a nearby flat, which had opened
stealthily to expose the interrogative head of an elderly
woman with cold cream masking her face. Anita gave Steve's
hand a tug and they moved on. 'I wouldn't be such a fool,'
she hissed, 'as to try taking him on singlehanded. Naturally
I'd fetch help.'

'And while you were fetching it, you'd be fighting him off
with a pair of nail-scissors? You must realize—'

'I took the phone into the hall cupboard and bedded
down with it there. The moment I heard anything, I'd have
dialled 999.'

'Oh, well. What a relief. And here was I thinking you'd
been a shade imprudent. Foolish me.' At the door to Anita's

flat, Steve snapped open the lid of the suitcase and peered inside. 'Blankets,' he reported, 'a pillow, a torch, and a packet of Parkside's wheatmeal digestive biscuits . . . untouched. A formidable armoury. Didn't you forget something? The aerosol spray? No smart female detective would dream of moving without it now, surely?'

'If you're going to be childish you can go back to your holiday essay and forget about coffee.' Holding the door open, she looked at him challengingly.

Steve blinked. 'Me—childish? I'm not sure who's running this conversation. At the very least, Anita, why didn't you ask me to go along with you? That would have been crazy, but only half as crazy.'

'You need your sleep, if you're working. I'm not working.' She stepped inside the flat. 'Coming in?'

He pursued her with a sigh. 'One of us needs their head examined. Maybe the pair of us. I'm not sure. It's too early in the day.' Reaching the living-room, he took her by the shoulders and steered her towards the sofa. 'Sit there and doze off while I do something about breakfast. Unless you get some rest—'

'I don't feel like resting, Steve. I'm too strung up. We can have some breakfast, by all means, and then I'd like you to do me a favour . . .'

'Drop dead and leave you alone?'

'Can you spare the time to drive me back to Elm Chase? I know you're busy—'

'I can finish off in ten minutes. After that I'm yours. Back to the house? You can't be there night and day, Anita. There's a limit to what you can take.'

'I only want to have a go at the neighbours. Ask around a bit.'

'The cops have done that.'

'I know, but they could easily have missed something. Or one of the residents might let slip an item of information that they wouldn't pass on to a uniform. It's worth a try.'

Steve made a woofing sound. 'And if I refuse to oblige? What will you do?'

She slipped him a wan smile. 'Go back by bus.'

In the car she sat still and silent: to Steve's best perception she was fast asleep. At the approach to a road junction, however, she stirred and spoke.

'If you turn left here, it's a quicker way through to the Chase and you miss the traffic lights.'

'Oak Avenue,' Steve remarked, eyeing the nameplate as he swung the wheel. 'Arboreal sort of district, by and large. Highly sought-after, as the estate agents have it. Crime waves don't form part of their vocabulary, I notice. Bad for business.'

'I used to collect acorns down here. When I had a bagful, I'd take them along to Auntie Maisie and she used to . . .'

Anita's voice trailed off. Contorting herself in the seat, she peered skywards through the car's side window. 'Slow down,' she urged, flapping a hand.

Steve braked. Craning her neck, Anita stared back at a tall, venerable, detached house on a corner site behind a stockade of overblown hedge and shrub. The property showed signs of considerable structural neglect. From the ungated access to the drive, the rear of a car slightly over- lapped the footway. The car, however, was not the object of Anita's attention. What she was looking at was the aluminium ladder mounted against the roof guttering at the side of the house. On a note of faint tension she said, 'Can you back up a bit?'

Reversing slowly, Steve came to another halt opposite the drive. From here was visible an angled section of the roof, on which a couple of human figures were crawling like beetles, wrenching pieces of slate away from the rafters and sliding them down into a gully. Having observed for a few moments, Anita said, 'Do they look like professionals to you?'

'They look like slobs. If I'd hired them to do that to my . . .' Pausing, he flung her a glance. 'Surely,' he objected, 'they wouldn't venture back to this neighbourhood? So soon?'

'Why not? If it's the same bunch, they might think it the smart thing to do. Like steering for the spot where the last shell exploded.'

They sat in silence, watching. The men seemed oblivious of them. After a while, Steve put the car back into gear. 'We can't stop here all morning. If you feel they should be checked out . . .'

'Hold on. I'm getting an idea.'

Steve sat patiently, keeping an eye on the rear-view mirror in case he obstructed traffic. Finally Anita emerged from trance. 'Could we forget about Elm Chase for the moment?'

'Sure. Where do you want to go instead?'

'The town centre. I'll show you where when we get there.'

To Anita's dismay, there was no sign at any of the tills of the dark cashier with the fancy spectacles. She approached another girl who was waiting for custom. 'I wonder, could you tell me . . .'

She stopped. Through the glass screen she had spotted the bespectacled girl at a desk in the rear office. 'Actually,' she resumed, a little breathless, 'I can see the person I want. The dark-haired young lady back there. Could I possibly have a quick word with her?'

Silently the cashier swivelled herself off her stool, plodded backstage. 'She'll be over in a minute,' she advised, returning. 'If you like to stand by that door . . .'

Anita waited. Presently the door opened and the dark girl appeared, smiling in recognition. 'You came in, didn't you,

the other day? Asking about Mrs Holwood. Has there
been—'

'I'm sorry to trouble you again,' Anita said urgently, 'but
I want to ask for your help. Can you possibly get away from
here for half an hour?'

'Now?'

'Yes. I'd like you to try and identify someone.'

'The fair-haired man,' the girl said astutely, 'who was
with Mrs Holwood?'

'Right. I think I know where he might be. Could you?'

'I'll have to get permission. Hang on a sec.'

She was back in a minute. 'I've fixed it with Mr Revis.
Told him my mother's poorly. She's not that good, so it's a
white lie. Where are we off to?'

'Not far. We've a car outside.'

Parked on a yellow band, Steve was looking about him
nervously for traffic wardens. Anita opened the rear door
for the cashier. 'I'm afraid I never asked your name . . .?'

'Linda. Linda Matthews.'

'This is Steve, and I'm Anita. Let's go, shall we?'

On the way back, Anita explained the situation. Linda
looked uncertain.

'I only saw him for a moment,' she reminded them. 'And
then I wasn't taking all that much notice. I do remember
he looked more like a city gent than a roofer. But then I
suppose he was off duty. Even so . . .'

'What we're hoping,' Steve told her, overtaking a bus, 'is
that you might recognize the guy in overalls. You've a good
memory, I hear, for names and faces.'

'Certain people I tend to recall,' Linda said modestly.
She seemed to be assuming that Steve belonged to the CID.
'I don't know about picking 'em out on a roof, though.
Tricky, isn't it?'

Reaching across to the glove-box, Steve extracted a
leather case which he passed to her. 'Binoculars. Good ones,

Jap-made. Came from Las Palmas. We thought maybe, if you stood on the far side of the street . . .'

'Won't he see me?'

'Stay inside the car, then.'

'I don't mind having a go.'

When they arrived back at the house in Oak Avenue, however, the roof was deserted. The ladder was still in place, and the car remained blocking the entrance. Anita gazed worriedly across the street.

'Tea break?' she surmised. 'Or perhaps they've done all they intend to—now they're pressurizing the occupant.'

'What do we do?' queried Steve. 'Wait a few minutes?'

Anita nodded. 'Let's give it a little while. If they're still around, we can't miss them when they show themselves again.'

CHAPTER 15

Attached in limpet fashion to the steep roof of the house owned by Sir Gerald Leigh-Ockenden, CBE, lately of White-hall and now in lonely retirement, Percy had spent the first hour in a cold sweat, figuring out a procedure and nerving himself to put it into effect.

Just a small shove at the right time . . .

Easy for Nigel to talk. He wasn't up there, clinging to any available handhold, rocked by a stiff breeze, feet skidding on damp slate, trying to stay within range of a partner who persistently strayed out of it while lifting sections of perfectly good roofing and disposing of them in the gully. For the sake of appearance, they had decided to replace an area of roughly eight square yards before calling it a day and charging Sir Gerald whatever magnitude of fee seemed extractable . . . despite his Civil Service record, the old man now had the appearance of one who in cerebral terms had passed his peak and was in free fall on the far side. Hundreds at least, was Nigel's confident prediction. Maybe a lot more. It depended on the state of Sir Gerald's bank balance and the degree of his dedication to home maintenance.

Dave seemed to be in more of a hurry than usual. Wordless, expressionless, he was using his claw-backed hammer as though it were electrified. To Percy he paid no attention whatever as the gap in the roof widened beneath their feet. Before long the two of them were seated, legs dangling, on the timbers, clearing away shattered remnants of slating, clawing out vestigial nails. And Percy was getting frantic.

The longer he delayed, the more impossible the task threatened to be. His nerve was starting to give. Something about Dave's sustained silence was oppressive, even though Percy was used to a high level of taciturnity on the part of his workmate. Instead of making it easier, the lack of communication between them was somehow adding to the problem.

Angrily, Percy took a grip of himself. This was the man, a yard or two from him, who almost certainly had behaved without scruple towards a fellow-creature of advanced years: he deserved to be snuffed out. The time for hesitation was gone.

'Know something, Dave?'

The chin of the younger man came up and round.

'I reckon,' Percy proceeded chattily, 'if you was to come round this side we could take off the rest of them slates between us in half a jiffy. Then fetch the new lot up here and be shot of the job. What say?'

Extracting a nail, Dave sent it clattering to the floor of the loft, part of which was now open to the heavens. 'Why not?'

Percy climbed cautiously to his knees. 'Get round here with us, then. Look sharp.'

'What's the big rush?'

The roof guttering stood out below them at the acutest of angles, reaching for the void. Percy swallowed. 'Wouldn't say no to a hand, to be honest. Feel a bit squiffy. Must be somethink I ate.'

From the far side of the chasm, Dave surveyed him. 'If you're figuring on flaking out, fall to your left. Unless you're looking for a headache.'

'Get across here and give us your arm, will you?'

Out of the corner of an eye, Percy could see that the street below was deserted. There had been a car which had braked to a halt, then backed up and hovered for a minute or so; but now it had gone. Pedestrians seemed to be non-existent. If the residents of Oak Avenue were in the habit of venturing out at all, evidently it was not at this time of the morning. With leg-muscles braced against the pitch of the roof, Percy passed a hand feebly across his eyes as Dave came lethargically to his haunches and made an initial movement in his direction.

'Stop where you are, then.'

Percy had no plans to go anywhere. He was in fact, he found to his chagrin, frozen to the spot, like the greenest of novices on a rock face. A gust of wind banged against him. He clutched at a rafter.

'Give us your hand. Which way d'you want to move?'

'Can't move . . .'

Reaching out, Dave clasped his upper arm.

Another sudden gust swayed the pair of them. Reeling backwards, Percy deliberately carried his weight on, felt the other's grasp slacken as he had known it would. Self-sacrifice was no part of Dave's nature. Regaining balance, Percy dived forward once more, fetched up heavily against his partner, who swore, fending him off. Yearning for some extra poundage, Percy launched himself a second time. Dave released a shout.

'Watch it, you bloody cretin!'

Something was wrong. This time, Percy met with no resistance. Dave had ducked clear. Arms flailing wildly, Percy went into an uncontrollable wobble at the very rim of the hole they had just created. For an instant, it was touch and go which way he toppled.

Fortune smiled. Beneath his right foot a slate cracked explosively, tilting him the opposite way from the guttering. With a wail, he dived neatly through the cavity.

'First incident of the kind we've had,' said Nigel, applying brisk massage to Percy's left thigh. 'Normally our safety record is something we're quite proud of. Always a first time, I suppose. How does that feel, old chap?'

Percy moaned.

'Badly shaken up, I dare say.' Sir Gerald Leigh-Ockenden came over with a tumbler of brandy, gave apprehensive scrutiny to Percy's recumbent form on the living-room couch. 'Lucky he fell into the attic and not the other way. Three floors would have been quite a drop.'

'Quite a drop,' Nigel agreed. To give vent to his inner fury, he glanced across at Dave who was looking on from the doorway. 'Wasn't there something you could have done?'

'Not down to me, is it? Them cross-rafters was rotted.'

Sir Gerald shifted uneasily. 'Hazard of the trade, I suppose?'

Nigel looked thoughtful. 'Depends on the terms of the contract, as applicable between customer and workforce. Generally speaking, you can say we wouldn't expect to be exposed to danger from a preventable cause of that nature, and furthermore . . .'

Twenty minutes later, Percy was pronounced fit enough to leave by car and was assisted out of the house. By that time, Nigel had renegotiated a settlement acceptable to all parties. Sir Gerald looked chastened, but at the same time relieved to be clear of liability. On the doorstep, Nigel turned.

'You'll have it in cash for us by tomorrow morning, then, Sir Gerald?'

'Without fail. You can rely on me. As my friends and colleagues would testify, I'm a man of—'

'While I'm running Percy to the hospital, Dave will stop on to tidy up on your roof.'

'That's most kind.'

'Don't want the rain seeping in, do we? A sound job and a finished job—that's our motto.'

'I'm sure it is.'

'I'll call back in the morning, around nine.'

'The money will be waiting for you. How much VAT did you say I was saving, for cash payment?'

'Getting on for a hundred,' Nigel said glibly. 'Worth a little extra time and trouble, isn't it, Sir Gerald? And a nice watertight property into the bargain, when Dave's finished up there. Dave, I'll be back for you in a couple of hours, okay? Give you time to seal everything off?'

Dave nodded.

'Mind you don't fall, as well,' implored Sir Gerald, with a mixture of waggishness and terror.

'Trust Dave. He's very sure-footed.' Nigel cast him a look of detestation before swarming behind the wheel of his BMW and engaging gear. 'See you later,' he announced through the open window. He glanced at Percy beside him. 'Straight home?' he inquired in an undertone.

'I reckon I should see a doctor.'

'You don't need a doctor. What you need is your head examined. How did you come to louse it up like that?'

'Tried me best,' muttered Percy, massaging his thigh tenderly. 'Anyway, you screwed the old codger for more than we was reckoning—can't be bad, can it?'

'It can . . . if we don't settle the Dave problem.' Letting

the clutch in forcefully, Nigel rocketed the car backwards into the street. Driving off, he and his associate were still arguing. For this reason, neither of them noticed the white Sierra saloon, containing three people, which pulled away from the kerbside farther up the road and settled in pursuit.

CHAPTER 16

'Don't lose him, for heaven's sake.'

'Easier said than done. He drives like a maniac.' Steve bit his lip, concentrating on roadcraft. 'This is no job for amateurs, if you ask me. We've got the car number. Why don't we just—'

'We can tell the police when we've something more concrete to go on.' Anita turned in her seat. 'You're positive, Linda, it's the same man?'

'Practically certain. It's the hair,' explained the cashier, leaning forward between the front seats to stare through the windscreen, 'and the build. Not to mention his clothes. I'd swear it's him.'

'Pushing his luck, isn't he?' Approaching an intersection, Steve jumped the lights to follow the BMW across. After he had done it, his stomach went on churning.

'Operating the same district, you mean, so soon?' Linda looked doubtful. 'If the price was right, he probably thought it was worth chancing.'

'What he didn't know,' Anita said tensely, 'was that Linda would be on the spot to identify him.'

Linda looked modest. 'What are you going to do now?'

'See where they're making for. Sorry we can't drop you off. If you get into hot water with your boss, tell him—'

'That's okay. I wouldn't miss this for the world. First time I've been in a car chase.'

'Welcome to the ranks,' Steve said wryly.

On the edge of town, the BMW turned off into a trailer park. Pulling up in a bus bay, Steve gave Anita a frowning look. 'What now? An invasion of privacy, or do we stick around here in the hope that—'

'Go in after him.'

'I think he's coming out again,' said Linda.

As the BMW emerged, they could see that it now contained only the driver. Accelerating after it, Steve remarked, 'He's dumped the little fellow, so now he's on his own. Where's he making for now?'

After another four miles the question was answered. On the approach to a built-up area, the car ahead swerved off the road once more to enter the forecourt of a new, raw, unlandscaped block of flats with the name BRIDLE COURT in neon lettering over the main entrance. Squealing to a standstill in a marked bay next to a red Jaguar, the driver got out. From where they had stopped at the roadside, Linda inspected him again through the binoculars. She gave a nod.

'It's him, I'm positive.'

'Go inside and park,' Anita told Steve.

'What if—'

'There's no risk. He can't know us from Adam.'

Driving in sedately, Steve chose a parking bay on the far side of the forecourt. By this time the driver of the BMW had vanished through the main entrance. Anita unclipped her seat belt.

'You two wait here.'

'Steady on, love. He might—'

'I must find out which apartment is his.'

She was off, trotting across the forecourt to the swing doors. Steve threw Linda a helpless glance.

'She'll be better on her own,' he muttered. 'Less conspicuous.'

'That's right. And anyway,' Linda said supportively, 'he should have no reason to think he's being watched. I mean he hasn't tried to throw us off, has he?'

'I'm not sure. He's done one or two crazy things, but it could be he's just a rotten driver.' Steve consulted the dashboard clock. 'Sorry about this, Linda. If you're not back by lunch-time, will they give you the push?'

'If they do, I'll claim unfair dismissal. I've not had a morning off since I joined.'

'How long is that?'

'Three months,' she said seriously.

Ten minutes blipped past on the digital clockface. During this time, one or two of the residents came out and drove away in their cars, but of Anita or her quarry there was no further sighting. Steve began to fidget.

'She shouldn't be this long.'

'What exactly was she planning to do?'

'You tell me. Find out which flat he occupies—if he does —and then maybe . . . I've no idea.'

They sat for another five minutes. 'I'm going inside,' Steve announced, finger on belt-fastening. 'There's no reason—'

Linda jogged his arm. 'Somebody's coming out.'

The fair-haired man reappeared, holding something. Striding back to the BMW, he opened a rear door and released his burden inside. It looked like a cat or a very small dog. Slamming the door, he returned hurriedly to the driving seat and activated the starter. As the engine fired, Anita erupted from the block entrance and sprinted across the asphalt.

'Keep after him,' she gasped, falling into her seat.

'Where's he off to this time?'

'How would I know? But he's got Ouncey with him.'

'Great-Aunt Maisie's pet?'

'No mistaking him. I recognized his yap.'

'So we're after the right guy.' Bouncing the Sierra back

on to the highway, Steve pushed it to the limit in an effort to catch up. The BMW was moving extremely fast. 'Okay, love, you were on target. But we're starting to get out of our depth. Shouldn't we now notify the cops?'

'No time.' Anita's gaze was clamped on the car ahead. 'If we stop to phone, we'll lose him. And now that Ouncey's involved . . .'

From the rear seat, Linda said on a mystified note to Steve, 'I thought you *were* the police?'

'What gave you that idea?'

'Well, the way you—'

'Keep your eyes on the road,' counselled Anita. 'We don't want to end up in a field.'

'Frankly, love, I'd as soon finish up there as a few other places I could mention. What were you doing inside the block, all that time?'

'I followed him upstairs to the second floor. He let himself in the door of number twelve and shut it behind him, so after a minute I tiptoed along and stood listening. That's when I heard Ouncey. He sounded frightened.'

'Poor little beggar.'

'Keep your foot down, he's gaining on you. Well, after a bit he stopped yapping and there was dead silence, so then I rang the doorbell . . .'

'You *what?*'

'Rang the doorbell. I thought he wouldn't answer, but he did. Eventually. He took so long, I'd had a chance to concoct some myth about canvassing for views on maintenance charges, pretending I was from the leaseholders' association, if such a thing exists. While I was blurting all this out I listened like mad, but there still wasn't another sound from inside. I tried to think of a way of getting myself invited in . . .'

'Did he seem suspicious?'

'Not unduly. Impatient, mostly.'

'Other things on his mind,' Linda suggested darkly.

'Quite. Like, had he given Ouncey enough tranquillizer? Because that's what I'm convinced he's done. Anyhow, after he'd closed the door on me I walked to the end of the landing and waited just round the corner. After a while he came out, carrying Ouncey, and went downstairs again. So I came down after them.'

'Is the dog . . .?'

'Oh, he was alive all right. Drowsy, but taking notice. I could see that from the top of the stairs. Question is,' Anita concluded, staring through the windscreen as the BMW went into a right-hand bend, 'where on earth is he taking him now?'

'For a walk?'

'What's wrong with the garden behind the block? If he wanted to—'

'Watch it,' Steve said suddenly. 'I'm turning left.'

The car ahead had already done so, wheeling in a screech of rubber to dive between yorkstone pillars marking the entrance to a public nature reserve. After fifty yards the access road broadened into a car park on the fringe of the territory, a gently undulating expanse of grassland and trees, latticed by footpaths and dotted with signposts. When they reached the gravelled rectangle, the fair-haired man was already locking the doors of his car and striding off towards a clump of firs, holding the dog under his arm. Anita thumped the dashboard with her fists.

'Don't let him get out of sight!'

'He's sure to spot us, love, if we crowd him. Let's give him a head start.'

As the man vanished beyond the trees, Anita flung open her door and jumped out. 'He's got Ouncey,' she wailed, taking off in pursuit.

'Anita! Come back here.'

Ignoring Steve's call, she hurried on. Steve threw up his

arms. 'Hang about,' he told Linda, who was looking on with an open mouth. 'If we're not back in twenty minutes, go for help.'

By the time he reached the firs, neither Anita nor the man was in view. The footpath fell sharply away to the right, winding between more conifers towards a lake which was visible below. From the crest, Steve caught a movement. It came from a point at the water's edge, away to his left: an intervening belt of rhododendrons partly obscured the sightline. It did not, however, act as a barrier against sound. Steve broke into a run.

Near the lakeside the path divided. Halting uncertainly, he chose the route that seemed to follow the bank, and as he darted along it he heard voices. One of them was Anita's, stressed to the limit. Rounding an outcrop of reeds, he came upon the two of them, locked in close embrace a yard or so from the water, lurching and rotating. Somewhere between them was the dog, its forepaws over the man's shoulder, its eyes red-rimmed and glazed. Steve hesitated.

Anita spotted him. 'Grab Ouncey!' she screamed.

Swung about, she was held with her back to the lake, arched perilously towards it. Humiliated by his own irresolution, Steve closed in.

At his first touch, to his astonishment, the man capitulated. Releasing Anita, he allowed the dog to half-jump, half-fall to the ground and blunder off. He himself stood passive, bent slightly at the knees, one arm encircling his face as though in expectation of an imminent and brutal cranial assault. 'Okay,' he puffed from behind the protective sleeve. 'You win. No need for . . . Let's talk, shall we? No need for . . .'

Anita swung a punch which connected with his right ear. 'He was going to drown Ouncey! He was just on the point of—'

'Who the blazes are you?' Nigel was looking at her dizzily.

'Grab his arms, Steve. Don't let him get away.'

'I'm not moving.'

Inclined to believe him, Steve nevertheless took the pre-
caution of doing as Anita requested. Beneath his well-cut
jacket, the arms of his captive felt alarmingly puny: there
was nothing of him, no bulk, no sinew, no fibre. Steve
experienced a surging return of self-confidence. On a physical level, this was someone he would find no difficulty in
handling. In his relief, he spoke with renewed assurance.

'Was that the plan? To get rid of the dog?'

'Listen, I can explain. I'm looking after it for a friend . . .'

'I'll just bet you are. A friend called Maisie Holwood?'

Nigel's jaw quivered. 'Who?'

'Oh, come *on*. You're not going to tell us you've never
met her?'

'Toss him in the lake, Steve. Hold him under the water.'

'What's eating this spitfire? Who does she think she is?'

Anita went for his eyes. With a bleat of dismay, Nigel
wrenched himself free, took two steps backwards, lost his
footing on the steep part of the bank, teetered briefly and
went in with a splash. Rising to the surface in a cloud of
bubbles, he thrashed the water. 'Help me!'

'Guess I'd better oblige,' Steve told Anita. Sliding to the
foot of the bank, he reached out for visible segments of
Nigel's fashionable upper garment, towed him in, then
hoisted him out. Seated forlornly on the mud and shingle,
Nigel wiped moisture out of his eyes and mouth while
shivering uncontrollably. Steve squatted to survey him. 'If
you don't want a repeat of the experience, I'd advise you to
come clean with us. Miss Blythe here has a vested interest
in causing you the maximum amount of discomfort.'

Nigel spat out a piece of water-lily. 'Keep her away,' he
choked. 'I don't know what's bugging her, but I can tell
you this—I never did the old lady any harm. It wasn't me.
I wouldn't—'

'You do know who we're talking about, then?'

'Lend us a handkerchief, will you?' Snatching it, Nigel dabbed at his features while keeping a wary eye on the looming figure of Anita on the bankside above him. 'Look here,' he went on, having cleared his throat a dozen times and wrung some of the water out of his jacket and slacks, 'as long as you get her to lay off, I'll tell you everything I know. I'm willing to cooperate. As a matter of fact, I was on the point of contacting the authorities—'

'Everything you know about what?'

'The Maisie Holwood business. That's what you're asking about, I assume.' He pointed to Ouncey, who was sitting at the lakeside ten yards from them with his eyes blearily half-shut. 'That's her pooch.'

'We know that. How did you come by him?'

'Dave handed him over. He—'

'Dave?'

'That's the name!' exclaimed Anita. 'The one Auntie Maisie mentioned to me. She as good as said he was threatening her.'

'She's her niece?' Nigel demanded of Steve. 'I might have guessed. Never get involved with relatives.' His teeth started to chatter. 'I'm going to catch my death, sitting here. Can't we get back to the—'

'In a moment. Tell us first what you know about this Dave. Is he the one we're looking for?'

'It must have been him. I'll be perfectly frank with you,' Nigel said with nauseating unction, 'we did try a little hard bargaining with Mrs Holwood on the basis that the job was a dodgy one and she'd made it plain that she had the capital to hand, but there was never any intention—'

'You went with her to the building society?'

'That's right, that was me. She seemed a bit unsure of herself, so not unnaturally I went along to give her moral support and a little financial advice, should she need it.

There was no pressure. We agreed a figure and she drew it
out. That's all it amounted to.'

'How cosy. We can enlarge on that later. The immediate
question is, where does Dave come into it? Did he go back
to the house by himself, later?'

'He must have done. To search for the money.'

'What money?'

'The nest-egg he was convinced your aunt must have
stowed away somewhere,' Nigel told Anita, shrinking fear-
fully as she made menacing forward movements. 'He did
say he was going back for it on the Sunday, but we never
imagined . . . He must have gone berserk.'

'That's one word for it,' Steve said icily. He glanced
across at Ouncey, who was now curled up on the bank, fast
asleep. 'What were you about to do with the dog, just now?'

'I brought him here for some exercise.'

'Oh yes? Water gymnastics?'

'Look, you sound like a reasonable couple. It must be
obvious to both of you that I—'

'Wouldn't be capable of lifting a finger against a fellow-
creature, even to save your own skin?' Steve pondered him.
'You'll have to allow us our own views on that. Feeling a
bit chilled?'

'Frozen to the bone.'

'What a pity,' Anita said softly into his right ear, causing
it to twitch. 'Auntie Maisie probably felt a bit uncomfortable, too. I wonder if she was given a chance to complain?'

'It was Dave, I tell you. We had nothing to do with—'

'Tell us all you know about Dave. We're listening.'

Nigel complied with some eagerness. At the end of his
recital Steve and Anita exchanged glances, and Steve gave
a slight nod. 'Where is he now?' he asked.

'Dave? At this minute? We left him at the old codger's
house in Oak Avenue, finishing off the job. He should still
be there. I said I'd call back for him later.'

'The job,' Anita repeated bitterly. 'What is it—half a dozen new slates at a thousand quid apiece? Same as for Auntie Maisie?'

'We charge the going rate,' Nigel declared righteously. 'It's dicey work. Plenty of risk involved. Only this morning, Percy hurt himself when he fell through into the attic. Our fees take account of the—'

'Oh, shut up.' Rising, Anita walked over to where Ouncey was lying and scooped him up. 'I'll see you back at the car,' she called, and made off.

Steve gave Nigel a prod. 'You heard what the lady said. Oh, and in case you were thinking of drying yourself off with a sharp sprint, forget it. I'm in fairly good shape, myself.'

At Steve's request, Linda took the wheel. 'I've not driven for a while,' she warned nervously, 'so you might have to put up with a few jerks.'

'They'll be nothing to the jerk I'm putting up with already.' Steve, none too gently, helped the semi-collapsed figure of Nigel into the rear seat, where he sat shivering between sneezes. 'Sorry to inflict this on you, Linda, but I'm taking no chances with this jellified mass of vocal protest. The sooner we hand him over, the happier I'll be.'

Anita sat silently with the oblivious Ouncey in the front. After a mile at a tentative pace, Linda said, 'There's a call-box. Shall I pull in?'

'I'll get through to Sergeant Bennett,' said Anita, squirming sideways to deposit the dog on the seat, 'and tell him we're on our way.'

'Good thinking, love. Tip him off about Dave. And you'd better ask him to lay on a blanket and a stiff brandy. We don't want our friend here pegging out from pneumonia. He still has a purpose to serve.'

Nigel moaned faintly, and sneezed again.

They waited while Anita made the call. 'You're to take him straight to the station,' she reported on her return. 'The chief inspector will be waiting to interview him. And he'll want statements from both of you.'

'Was it Davison you spoke to?' inquired Steve.

'No, Sergeant Bennett.' Reclaiming Ouncey, Anita nodded to Linda, who with slightly increased assurance got the car back into its stride. Steve leaned forward.

'What about Dave? Do they have anything on him?'

'I didn't wait to find out. I said we'd be back as soon as we could. Bennett wants you to drop me off in Oak Avenue,' she added, 'so that I can call at the house and tip Sir Gerald off.'

'Tip him off?' Steve echoed, perplexed.

'About Dave. In case he tries something.'

'For Christ's sake, love. That's their job. Can't they call him, or send a patrol car?'

'They don't want to put Dave on his guard. He might be up on the roof, but if he's not . . .'

'Does Bennett realize what he's asking of you?' Steve demanded angrily. 'This guy's a killer. What if he gets another of his impulses?'

'I can handle it, Steve. We discussed it, the sergeant and me. I know how to avoid arousing his suspicion.'

'Just the same, I think he should . . . How about the dog?'

'I'll take Ouncey with me. Leave him with one of the neighbours, probably. I know a few of the people around there.'

Dissatisfied but irresolute, Steve sat back. Beside him, Nigel glided a smile of faint malice in his direction. 'Stubborn young person, isn't she? Quite fond of going her own way. I'd look out for myself, old son, if I were in your shoes.'

'Why hullo, Nigel.'

Arriving belatedly in the front office from the street,

Sergeant Bennett surveyed with evident surprise the blanket-wrapped figure shivering in a chair by the counter while his captors murmured with the duty sergeant. At his appearance they all turned. 'What's this?' he inquired of Steve. 'A citizen's arrest?'

'If that's what you like to call it.' Steve gestured at the chair. 'One suspect, Sergeant, delivered fairly intact as requested. Minus only his permanent wave and his dignity. He's all yours.'

Bennett looked blank. 'Who was it did the requesting?'

Steve blinked. 'You did, as I understand. Isn't that what you told Anita . . . Miss Blythe?'

'Miss Blythe? I've not spoken to her.'

'An hour or two ago,' Steve protested. 'On the blower.'

'Not me, chum. I'm only just back from a robbery. Talking of which—how's tricks, Nigel, these spring days?'

'I'm wet and I'm freezing. You took your time getting here.'

'Contrite apologies. I had a hysterical burgled housewife to cope with. One thing I'll say for you, Nigel: you've generally gone about things in a rather subtler way, if that's a recommendation. Lots of malleable suckers still around? Let's see now. What was it? Phoney insurance, am I right? Or did you graduate from that? Phantom trade directories?'

'I'm in the roofing business,' Nigel affirmed with dignity.

'The *roofing* business?'

After a pause for reflection, Sergeant Bennett took Steve to one side. 'You're not suggesting this tailor's dummy is responsible for what happened to Maisie Holwood? Nigel's been around as a small-time operator for years. We've never thought of him as potentially violent. I doubt if he could swat a fly.'

'We're not fingering him for Maisie. It's an associate of his. The guy you want,' Steve said, speaking rapidly, 'goes by the name of Dave Forester, who as far as we know is at a house in Oak Avenue right now. And unless you move fast, Sergeant, Anita could be finding herself in a heap of danger, right this minute.'

CHAPTER 17

Having knocked, Anita transferred Ouncey to her other arm and waited.

Presently the door opened partially to reveal glimpses of a tall, elderly man with rimmed glasses perched on a beak of a nose, and an expression of remote severity. 'If it's double-glazing,' he told her, 'or something of that nature—'

'I'm not selling anything,' said Anita. 'I just wondered if I could get a message to the man working on your roof. Is that possible?'

Sir Gerald responded to her smile. 'I don't see why not. You're somebody connected with the firm?'

'No. No connection.'

'I see.' Sir Gerald looked baffled. 'A message, you say?'

'Yes. Could you ask him whether he's lost a dog.'

'Lost a dog . . . Very well. I'll have to go upstairs and call to him from the attic. Would you mind waiting a few moments? You'll forgive me if I don't ask you in. I have a cat who rather objects to other animals encroaching on her preserves.' He peered fussily at the dog, supine in the crook of Anita's elbow. 'It's quite sheltered here inside the porch. I'll be back directly.'

'It's most kind of you.'

Tickling Ouncey's fringe, Anita leaned against the porch windowframe, glancing out now and then at the front garden and the street, which remained quiet. A minute or so elapsed. Finally a rattling sound came from the door as a

preliminary to its swinging back to release into the porch a
tawny-haired young man in pale blue overalls. His face wore
a slight frown which deepened momentarily at sight of
Ouncey, before vanishing entirely to be replaced by an air
of indifference.

'You asking about a dog?'

'That's right. This one.'

Ouncey had awoken to stare intently at the newcomer. A
faint, bubbling growl came from his throat. Anita held him
closer. 'Does he belong to you, by any chance?'

Dave shook his head. 'Never seen it before.'

'You're quite sure? I was told you might be the new
owner.'

The frown returned. 'Who told you that?'

'It's not important.'

Behind Dave, inquisitively within earshot, the shuffling
figure of Sir Gerald was dimly visible inside the hall. Pulling
the door to behind him, Dave advanced further into the
porch. 'Where'd you find him?'

'If he doesn't belong to you, that's not important either.'

'Somebody must've put you on to me.'

'That's right.' Her eyes met his. 'Always somebody, isn't
there?'

Dave's dirt-streaked right hand came up to administer a
jerky scratching of his neck. 'Next street along, was it?'

'Was what?'

'Where they put you on to us.'

'What makes you think so?'

'Just guessing.'

Anita took a pace or two towards the exit. 'If he's not
yours, I'd better take him to the police. They might have a
record of his getting lost.'

'Hang about . . .' Dave's hand came away from his neck
to restrain her. 'I might be interested. Always wanted a
dog.'

'Oh really?'

'Come outside and let's have a proper look at it.'

Standing on the mud-and-gravel surface of the drive, Anita held Ouncey for examination. Dave extended a finger, from which the dog shrank noticeably. 'Not too friendly, is he? What's his problem?'

'You're the one, Dave, with the problem.'

He stared at her. 'Who told you my name?'

'A friend of yours.'

'How'd you bump into him?'

'Did I say it was a he?'

Dave began to stutter. 'If you c-can't give us a name, there's no p-p-p . . .'

'Come on,' Anita said coolly. 'Let's not haggle, Dave. You know all about Ouncey here, don't you? Maisie gave him to you.'

'Maisie? Who might she be, when she's at home?'

Anita restored the dog to its former posture. 'Not at home any more, is she, Dave?'

'I dunno what you're on about.' He was making no move to return to the porch.

'You did a job, didn't you? For my Great-Aunt Maisie. On her roof. And she asked if you'd like to take Ouncey because she couldn't look after him any more.'

'I do jobs for a lot of people.'

'You must remember my Auntie Maisie. Elm Chase, just round the corner. She told me about you. Said you'd taken a real shine to Ouncey and she hoped you'd be able to look after him better than she had.'

'She said that?'

'So you see, you don't have to pretend not to recognize him. Now that Auntie Maisie's gone, he's legitimately yours. You know she was attacked, a day or two later?'

'Oh yeh?'

'Being so old, of course, she couldn't put up much of a

fight. I'd have thought you'd have seen it in the papers.'

'I don't read the papers.'

'Can't say I blame you. Full of crime, aren't they, and violence? Poor old Auntie M, she really came up against it. Still, that's how it is, these days. I don't suppose they'll ever catch who did it. But I'm right, aren't I, Dave? It was you she gave Ouncey to?'

'You've got it wrong. I never met the lady.'

'Nigel says you did.'

'Who's Nigel?'

'Seeing what happened to my great-aunt, I can understand you being cautious, but there's no need, Dave—honestly. It was just coincidence. And I'd like you to have Ouncey. I can't take him myself, because I live in a flat.'

'Sorry. Can't help you.'

'Well, can I ask another favour? When you're finished here, could you possibly come round to my great-aunt's house and take a look inside the roof for me?'

'What's wrong with it?'

'Nothing, as far as I know. It's just that there might be something hidden in the joists of the attic, only I can't get up there to search. It needs an expert. I don't want to call in anybody I know, because . . . It's a question of probate. I'm sole beneficiary, you see. And there's inheritance tax to consider. If I can keep the declared amount below a certain figure . . .'

Dave studied her. 'What is it you reckon you're after?'

'If we trace it, you'll find out.' Anita moved nearer to him. 'Confidentially, Dave, there could be quite a bit in it for you. I don't mind paying for results, as long as you're prepared to keep them under your hat. What do you say?'

Excitement built up inside Dave's chest as he followed the girl through the front door into the frigid hall of Maisie Holwood's house.

Any loitering doubts about this great-niece of the old bat's had been dispelled as they came along. In her quiet way, she was frantic to get at the loot: anyone could see that. He could scarcely believe his luck. Here he was with a miraculous second chance . . . he mustn't blow it this time. The attic. Why hadn't he tried the attic? Because there hadn't been time. The tempting Bella had taken his mind off things. Now it was different. He had a head start, and it wasn't going to be wasted.

Closing the door, the girl turned to face him. 'I don't know exactly where the box is hidden. I rather doubt whether Auntie Maisie did any more. Her husband put it there years ago, as a kind of insurance. Just before he died he told me about it, but he didn't specify the spot. All I know is, it's somewhere up there in the attic ceiling. It's too high for me to reach, and I can't manage the ladder.'

Dave nodded with apparent placidity. 'A box, you say?'

'Or it might be a leather bag. A container of some sort.'

'I'll find it, don't you worry. You'd better show us the way.'

Still carrying the dog, she mounted the stairs ahead of him. On the second landing she turned to him again. 'You'll need this,' she said, handing him a steel bolt from a small chest in the centre of the floor. 'Twist it inside that hole in the ceiling and then you can lift the trapdoor. There should be a ladder just inside.'

Stepping on to the chest, Dave followed directions and knocked the trapdoor up with the butt of his hand. The ladder was there, as she had said. Hauling it down, he fixed it in place and climbed up to the opening, leaving the bolt where it had been lying. From inside the attic he peered back.

'So, where's the best place to start?'

'Far corner, left-hand side. I think that's what my great-uncle said, though I might have got it wrong. Worth a try, anyhow. You did say you had a torch?'

Removing it from the pouch of his overalls, Dave aimed the beam at the attic ceiling.

'If you look closely,' the girl called from below, 'you might see a patch of plaster a different colour from the rest. He did say he'd knocked a lump away, stowed the container inside and then replastered. See if you can spot it.'

Hoisting the ladder from its position by the trapdoor, Dave positioned it in the left-hand corner and climbed the rungs to the top. His movements were becoming a little feverish. The torchlight showed him only an expanse of crazed, heavily stained plasterwork, devoid of distinguishing marks. With his knuckles, he tried tapping various places. All of them sounded hollow.

'I'll need to cave in the lot,' he called down.

'Okay.' Her voice sounded remote.

Seizing the light hammer he always carried while working, Dave attacked the ceiling from the corner outwards. Plaster fell in noisy showers to the floorboards. When he had a sizeable hole, he felt inside. His fingertips met unplaned timbers and slating. Finding nothing else, he moved on, enlarging the destruction.

'Zilch in the corner,' he reported. 'I'm working to the right.'

No reply came from below. She'd be holding her breath, tensed for word of a discovery. She'd be tenser still, he thought cynically, if she knew of the plans he had for her. First things first. The hammerhead oscillated to the movements of his wrist, disintegrating the plaster in a broadening swathe. Now and then he paused to feel around with his free hand, alert for the touch of tin or leather or canvas.

Presently he suspended the operation. What with the exertion and the plaster dust, working conditions inside the

attic were deteriorating fast. Visibility, too, was worsening.
The dust-cloud hung about him, blocking such light as there
was from the landing. Coughing, he turned his head.

'Can you switch a few more lights on down there?'

Again there was silence. Scowling, Dave descended a
rung or two, peered through the man-made fog. He could
see no glimmer at all from the landing. He went lower,
below cloud-level: still darkness. He aimed the torch.

'Hey! What did you shut the hatch for?'

Sliding hastily the rest of the way, he crossed the flooring
to the trapdoor and grabbed the cross-members. When
he tugged, nothing happened. The square of woodwork
remained obstinately in its seating. With a curse, he took
up a new position directly above, gave it a mighty wrench,
to no avail.

'Turn the catch, will you? It's fastened itself.'

The ghostly silence persisted. Filling his lungs with the
polluted air, Dave bawled at the top of his voice. 'Hey there!
Can you hear me? This bloody thing is stuck. Get it open,
can't you?'

He stamped on the floorboards. 'Come back here! I want
to get out.'

Her voice, when it responded, sounded strange. Thinner,
more metallic, as though stripped of a casing of insulation.
'Did Auntie Maisie say anything like that?'

'Twist the catch, you stupid cow.'

'Tell me about her, first. Did she ask you to let her go?'

'I don't know what you're raving on about. If you don't
bloody free this catch . . .'

'Yes, Dave? What will you do?'

He crouched wordlessly, breathing hard. Now she really
had it coming to her. Instead of the quick dispatch he had
planned, he would take considerable pleasure in devising
something more protracted. She deserved nothing less, the
lying bitch.

First, though, he had to get out. With the aid of the torch he located the hinged side of the trapdoor. The steel butts were mostly buried inside the seating, but Dave was used to worse than that. Unluckily he hadn't a chisel on him. The hammer, however, was claw-backed: he should be able to make do with that.

Reversing the head, he brought the spikes down hard, gouging the timber.

It was more solid than he had anticipated. Gasping for fresh air, he assaulted it repeatedly, once getting the claw so firmly lodged that he feared it would break as he wrenched it out. Gradually he created a ragged gap around one of the hinges. It was slow, painfully exhausting labour. How long had he been up here? What was the girl doing now?

As he turned his attention to the other hinge, Dave's nostrils started to twitch.

CHAPTER 18

Sir Gerald Leigh-Ockenden sounded as disorientated as he looked. 'Seem to be in demand this morning,' he mumbled to the inquisitorial figure of Detective Chief Superintendent Malling standing in the porch. 'Not used to all these comings and goings. First it's the men: then the young woman: now . . .'

'It's the lady, sir, we're interested in. Did she leave here by herself, do you know?'

'Now that I couldn't . . .' Sir Gerald paused maddeningly to ponder. 'She was talking to the workman, that I do know. She'd come about a dog. I left them to it, of course, out here on the driveway. After a bit I assumed she'd gone off. Then the young fellow stuck his head round my living-room door . . .'

'Forester? Was that his name?'

'Never did hear what they called him. Ah, wait a bit. Dave. I believe I did hear him addressed as Dave. Anyway, he said he had to be off, but he'd be back later to finish off my roof. Next thing, I heard this door slam. Whether or not the girl went along with him . . .'

Malling wheeled. 'Shove out a call, Frank, will you?'

Sergeant Bennett returned swiftly to the patrol car.

'You overheard nothing of their discussion, then?' the Chief Superintendent demanded of Sir Gerald, who looked shocked.

'I'm not in the habit,' he pointed out mildly, 'of listening in to people's conversations. Though in actual fact,' he added, as Malling was about to put another question, 'when I was passing through the hall on my way to the living-room, I did catch a word or two which made me wonder.'

'Wonder, sir?'

'I got the impression they were a bit at loggerheads about the dog. Its ownership. But I can't say for certain.'

'One more thing, sir. When the workman went off, was he driving a van or a car?'

The vagueness of Sir Gerald spilled over into total speechlessness. Malling said desperately, 'Can you remember how he arrived?'

'I *think* they all turned up in a car . . .'

'That's probably right,' Steve intervened. He had been hovering anxiously at the Chief Superintendent's elbow. 'According to Nigel Sharpe—or Murphy, whatever he calls himself—the van was a write-off after Forester crashed it on the Birmingham road. I forgot to tell you that.'

'So they all came here in Sharpe's car. And that's now languishing in a nature reserve.' Malling turned to Chief Inspector Davison on his other side. 'What d'you reckon, Bryan.'

'If he hasn't got transport, sir, things may be less ominous than we suppose. The girl may not be with him after all. On the other hand, if she's not, why has she disappeared?'

'Maybe she's tailing him, wherever he's gone. She seems keen on DIY investigation.'

'Yes, but there's another possibility. We've no proof—'

'Mr Malling.'

The Chief Superintendent turned tolerantly. 'Yes, Mr Walsh, what is it?'

'I've had an idea,' Steve said urgently. 'Maisie Holwood's house is only a short distance from here. What if they both went round there?'

'Why the blazes would they do that?'

'Anita tricked us into leaving her here to confront Forester. So I guess she had something worked out. And I've just remembered . . .'

'Remembered what?'

'A remark she made, just after we found her great-aunt. Whoever was responsible, she said, she'd like to get him into a room and *do things* to him.'

Malling gazed for a moment. 'Does she still have a key to Mrs Holwood's house?'

'Yes, she does.'

'Get round there, Bryan, double sharp. Take Todd and Bartholomew with you. All right, Mr Walsh, you go along too. I suppose there's no stopping you.'

The matter was no longer in doubt. It was smoke.

In mid-strike with the hammer, Dave paused to cough and choke. Apart from the fumes, vast globs of panic were starting to accumulate inside his chest and stomach. He could scarcely breathe for them. Forcing himself back to the task in hand, he glared in despair at the hinges. Neither was yet fully exposed. In sudden indiscriminate fury he rained blows on them, achieving no hint of movement.

'Enjoying yourself, Dave, up there?'

'Wait till I'm out of here. I'll kill you.'

'I'm sure you mean that. Quite the expert, aren't you, Dave, when it comes to killing?'

'You don't scare me.'

'That hardly seems necessary. You're doing quite a good job on yourself. About how long, Dave, would you estimate you've got?'

'We'll make a deal. I'll explain what happened about Maisie. In return, you'll put a hose on that fire . . .'

'Just when I've got it nicely alight? What a waste of Auntie Maisie's paraffin. I had to use practically all of it.'

'You can't do this. You're crazy. There's no way—'

A spasm of uncontrollable coughing drove Dave away from the trapdoor to find refuge on the far side of the attic, where so far there was more plaster dust than smoke. Crouched in the angle between roof and floor, he fought to clear his lungs and his brain. Presently he regained his voice.

'Don't you want to hear about your aunt?'

'My *great*-aunt. Not from you, thanks.'

'How d'you know it was me? How can you be sure?'

'I'm sure.'

'All right. It was me. I'll take the rap for it. That satisfy you?'

'You're taking the rap, Dave. Now, this minute. You've nothing to bargain with.'

'Who's bargaining? You're forgetting something. I can smash a way out of here any time I—'

Dave's voice soared to a screech. The crackling sounds beneath the floorboards had been drowned by a sudden 'Whoomph', followed immediately by an irruption of orange flame into the attic, engulfing the trapdoor area and licking up to the roof. For an instant he stared at it, aghast, limb-locked.

Recovering mobility, he got to his feet, staggered across to the ladder. Using one arm to shield his face from the heat, he scaled the rungs, stood blindly at the top and made feeble prods with the hammer at the underside of the slating. It bounced a little. His strength was ebbing. He couldn't ventilate. Flame seared his ankles.

'Get us out of here,' he sobbed. 'I don't want to die . . .'

Mounting another rung, he held the hammer poised.

As they drove up Elm Chase, Steve pointed through the windscreen. 'Look!'

Smoke and flame were billowing from the roof of Maisie's house. Chief Inspector Davison said, 'God Almighty . . .'

Before the driver had brought the car to a skidding halt alongside the porch, Steve was out and hurling himself impotently against the front door. He pounded the knocker. 'Anita!'

From somewhere to his left came a shattering of glass. Quitting the porch, he saw Davison and his uniformed colleagues hauling themselves across the sill of a broken ground-floor window. Pursuing them, he gained entry to a square room with its remaining furniture under dust sheets, eerily silent as though awaiting guests who had long since indicated their intention never to arrive. The inner door gave access to the hall. From here, a sustained crackling was audible. Ahead of Steve, the chief inspector was launching himself at the staircase in pursuit of the constables. 'Stay back, son,' he advised from midway.

Ignoring the injunction, Steve reached the first landing at his heels and then stopped, appalled. The entire floor above them was a mass of flame, roaring skywards. At the foot of the stairway leading to it, the constables stood in helpless attitudes, screening their faces from the heat. Davison glared round.

'Get back! There's nothing we can do. Call the fire brigade.'

Returning to the hall, Steve stood numbly for a moment,

struggling to focus his brain. Fire brigade. Telephone. There was no sign of an instrument. Recalling something, he opened the door of the hall cupboard and found it on the floor inside. Having made the call, he replaced the phone on the hall table and went on through to the living-room.

Anita sat crouched in Maisie's chair, fondling Ouncey's ears. At her feet stood a plastic can reeking of paraffin, although it was empty. She took no notice of Steve as he approached. Before he could say anything, however, she spoke herself, calmly, on a conversational level.

'Well, Steve. I think we made quite a decent job of that, don't you?'

Gently he took her hand. 'Come on, love. Let's have you out of here.'

She came unprotestingly to her feet. Ouncey lay shivering in her arms. Back in the hall, Steve steered her close to the nearer wall to avoid the blazing fragments that were starting to plummet from the stairwell, setting fire to sections of the carpet. They reached the porch without mishap. Outside, Davison's voice could be heard on the patrol car's radio. '. . . urgent need of medical attention. Request ambulance. Over.'

A squawk responded unintelligibly. Steve took Anita across to the vehicle. 'Mind if she sits in?'

Davison gestured assent. Installing herself without fuss in the rear seat, Anita looked out at what could be seen of the garden in the absorbed manner of a tourist visiting a stately home. At the cessation of the squawk, the chief inspector fired the engine and reversed the car to the gateway and out into the street.

On the far side, onlookers were assembling in groups. Other faces peered from nearby doors and windows. Continuing to back up for fifty yards, Davison finally halted the car at the kerbside and sat in silence for a while, observing the blaze as it steadily blanketed the roof. Presently, without stirring, he remarked, 'I suppose you might say he was lucky.'

'Who was?' Steve had an arm across Anita's shoulders, his fingers helping to soothe the dog.

'Unless he's got internal injuries, he should be okay. The fact that he—'

'You're talking about Forester? Did he get out?'

The chief inspector glanced across a shoulder. 'Dropped out, would be nearer the mark. He jumped off the roof.'

Steve felt Anita's body give a twitch. He tightened his grip. 'You're telling us he fell three storeys and got away with it?'

'A branch of a tree broke his fall, he says. Then he landed on a pile of bracken. Compound leg fracture, I fancy, plus a few ribs and this and that . . . but he's conscious and talking. My blokes are with him till the ambulance gets here.'

Steve sat digesting the news. Anita had become still again. Davison twisted his neck further to look back at her.

'Quite lucky for your girlfriend, too. Not that she isn't in a whole heap of trouble, as it is. Attempted murder is just one of the charges that'll be on the file. Why couldn't she leave it alone? We'd have got to Forester. He's already on a drink-driving rap, they tell me. *And* causing death. We'd have got to him.'

'Eventually,' Steve retorted. 'After he'd had time to create a bit more mayhem. At least Anita managed to cut a few corners for you.'

'She'd have done better leaving it to us. When will people learn that they can't casually take the law into their own hands? Now, I'm afraid . . .'

'What's going to happen to her?'

Davison grimaced. 'In the well-tempered phrase, that's for the court to decide. She'll go down, you know. Not much question about that.'

'Surely they'll take into account the—'

'Oh, due regard will be paid to all the circumstances, you can rely on that. Where's that bloody fire service?'

As he spoke, a two-tone cacophony proclaimed the arrival of the first appliance. Suspending conversation, Davison turned back to watch the activity. The bulk of Steve's attention remained nervously with the girl seated next to him: she seemed asleep or semi-conscious. Ouncey had buried his face in her jacket. Bracing himself for an unforeseen reaction, Steve gave her the slightest of nudges.

'Whatever happens, love, I'll still be around when they're through with you. And I'll look after Ouncey. That's a promise.'

She stirred, sighed, sat up straighter. 'You'll have to promise me something else, as well.'

'What's that?' His secret relief was huge, almost uncontainable.

'As soon as I'm available, you'll let me do something about your hair.'